Even My Bones

Cooper, Alayna, Author
Even My Bones
Alayna Cooper

ISBN: 979-8-218-93439-2

NOVEL

For information, email am.cooper3791@gmail.com.

Cover Art By:

Ed-Macy Herring

Interior Art By:

Tori Davis

To Steve-
sometimes all you need to be a good teacher
are encouraging words
and cool socks.

EVEN

MY

BONES

"**Human decomposition** is a natural process involving the breakdown of tissues after death. While the rate of human decomposition varies due to several factors, including weather, temperature, moisture, pH and oxygen levels, cause of death, and body position, all human bodies follow the same four stages of human decomposition."

- Aftermath Services (Specialists in Trauma Cleaning & Biohazard Removal)

1

AUTOLYSIS

Hi!
You're dead now. Isn't that fun?
Your body is already right on schedule. Your muscles
are stiffening. Your eyes have an… odd look to them.
Someone should close them for you.
It's going to be a while until we get where we want to be.
But that's okay. It's the journey, not the destination,
right? Ha, ha! You will get there, and it will be
wonderful.

Look, the paramedics are here! They even have a
stretcher for you! That's really quite nice of them. Seems
like things are moving along.

Wonderful.

[GOD] Are you listening?

[PATRICK] I should be asking you that, shouldn't I?

The sound that emits is GOD chuckling. It is a strange, and otherworldly sound. Not meant for ears at all.

[PATRICK] So, you're really here, then.

[GOD] I'm always here. I was here when the first ships set sail unto the seas and the first planes into the clouds. When the light of each star extinguishes, when the worms emerge after rain, when blood spills and taints the skin of the earth. I was there when you crawled from the womb and I'll be here when you return to the womb of a dark and buried coffin.

[PATRICK] I plan on being cremated, actually.

GOD laughs.
PATRICK covers his ears.

he has gentle eyes,
oh, oh,
gentle eyes.

Even My Bones

I was standing at the window today. It was hot. Summer, you know. Someone rode their bike out on the sidewalk and fell. They skinned their knee. I probably should have gone down to help, but I didn't. They were sitting on the ground for a while, just letting it bleed. I felt like it was something I shouldn't have been watching.

I also saw something weird at the edge of the woods. At first, like, I thought it must be a bear. But it wasn't. It was sniffing along the garden, and giant mushrooms were growing from its back. Giant mushrooms intertwined with its fur, all kinds, and it had more legs than it should have had... but it was evening, so it was getting hard to see.

There was a blood-moon tonight. I hear that's like, a sign of evil or something. I don't know.

There's a lot of things I feel like I shouldn't see.

Even My Bones

Wait, please. Wait.

The green light shimmers
(sour candy, beeping monitors, the numbers on the
microwave that spins, spins, spins your artificial meal
that will sit like lead in your stomach)
The stars have never been brighter, under here, under the
sky that never ends and is always, always beyond.

Will you cry with me under the evergreen?
(tears are sometimes joy)
Will you take my hand as if we are children, and smile as
happiness fills your chest so much it aches?
(your hands are warmer than mine)
Everything is okay. Everything is okay and I'll read to
you as you fall asleep.
(you sound like my mother)

Come on, just wait a second.

Lean on me. Lean on me,
and we'll watch the stars.

Even My Bones

my soulless ship is sinking

over winds and depths unblinking

the choir is lost,

on ears of frost,

my hollow lungs are clinking

Organs grow from trees.
They hang down like heavy oranges, like apples
drooping along branches, like succulent peaches that
burst with sweet juice when teeth breach them.
With each passing gust of wind
they seem to breathe, to function.
Blood leaks from cracks in the bark like sap.
It is thick and dark.
The sky is tinged in blurry hues of red above rustling
forest growth. Perhaps, if you were to get closer, you
might stop and stare. You might lower your axe and
scratch at the collar of your flannel that's suddenly too
warm. You might let your curiosity get the better of you
and raise your axe to the trunk, blistering the bark,
indenting the wood- and maybe, just maybe, inside the
tree there would be a writhing mess of innards and flesh
that makes you squirm.
The organs, they pulse,
and the light of eternity beckons.

Sunday morning. Church bells are ringing, and my leg is
wrapped in newspaper. I am newspaper boy.
Newspaper boy, the old woman chimes. Her voice is a
bell. Her voice is not real. Her voice is wrinkled.
Newspaper boy, are you hungry? She walks over to me,
glancing once at my leg, twice at the stain on my t-shirt.
She holds out a brown paper bag. It is leaking.
My stomach growls. Take it, it says. Take it because you
are hungry. Take it, you fucking glutton. Take it.
My hand is thin, it is formed of paperclips and drywall,
but I take it anyway, straining under the weight. When
the old woman is gone, and I've punched my stomach
into submission, I open the bag. It is dark. It is silly.
It is newspaper.
I grab it by the handful, yellowing and outdated, and
shove it into my mouth. My teeth scream. They are tired,
from the gum. I ignore them.
Good riddance, my stomach says. Good riddance.

Does it hurt? Am I hurting you? Is anything real, and if it
is, can we go outside and scream and wave our arms
around maniacally until lightning strikes us?
Are you real?
Are you sure?

Even My Bones

She takes my head in her hands, removes it from my
shoulders lovingly, and her eyes are teal mist and her
wings are that of a sparrow.
Free, free, free, she chants, her citrus tongue lapping out
like a snake. Free, free, free.

And the arms on my body wave around in joy, for I have
had nothing to give her, my wallet was empty. My
wallet, in my jeans, on my body that dances without me.

I crack a smile, like a broken egg, sure that what is
happening is good, sure that it is right. There is a galaxy
in her mouth and she uses it to kiss my forehead, crack
my skull. Blood pours out but it is not blood it is thick
and gelatinous and the hue of a grapefruit; my skull is
not bone but shell; and from my brain pops a tiny baby
sparrow.

Free, she chants, as my body claps and dances.
Free, free, free.

You are three years old.
You've discovered the wonders of wooden alphabet
blocks- painted yellows, and greens, and blues.
Ah, there's a red one!
You pick it up. Your mother is in the other room on the
phone, and the sun is large, and you can't understand her
voice yet. If you could,
you would know that she's saying,
*"I just don't know what to do. Mom, I don't know. I can't
raise a kid alone. It's- it's so hard. Mom, it's so hard."*
But you don't know that, you silly goose.
You don't know anything. You're three.
And the sun is very large.

Even My Bones

static

REPORTER: Good morning, [YOUR MIND]! As our motto goes, be bright! Be bright and silver, like the moon, for the moon, serve the moon. Serve… eternally. It totally won't smite you if you don't. Welcome to your local news station, I'm reporting live from… well, you don't care. You're dead.

Today a body was found in the lake. According to an eyewitness on his morning walk, the body was floating in the middle of the foggy water, unmoving. The eyewitness, Jerry Carson, watched as the body rose out of the wretched, algae filled water and began to cough up bits of paper- even pulling some (mucus-covered) from their nose and (wax-covered) from their ears.

"It was simply terrifying," Jerry stated in his interview with the press. "I'd never seen so many paper shreds in my life- unless you're counting the dumpster behind the office supply store."

What a mystery. What was the body doing in the lake? Have the authorities managed to capture it? And more importantly, what documents are the employees at the office supply store shredding? Personally, I think it's the birth certificates of immortal government agents, but you never know.

As usual, if you hear or see anything suspicious, like office-supply store employees outside during the day, contact the police immediately.

chop the hands that borne you,

tie the tongues that sang,

the lullabies of summer

don't ever

take the blame.

In the schoolbus, it's weak and yellow, bump after bump on a road no one can see (it is under us, the children). Weak and yellow sunlight on my band aids, from recess, from a boy called the Tiger. He pushed me down, the girls said he liked me, but that is not what I want. What I want is not weak, and it is not yellow, it is Tiger's fur brushed so his head looks good over my fireplace. And I will cover him in band-aids, choo-choo trains and firetrucks, dinosaurs and smiley faces, over and over and over I will cover him. Band-aid after band-aid, just to see how he likes it. The schoolbus bumps, one-two-three, and it is weak, and yellow, on a road nobody can see.

[GOD] What have you done?

PATRICK steps away.

[PATRICK] You don't like it?

The deer is dead. It lays on itchy grass under a pale sun and the hunting rifle's nose is pointed at the ground.

[PATRICK] I'm going to eat it.

[GOD] I made all the creatures, from the tiny mouse to the roaring lion. I made all of them. Death is life and life is death and sometimes I manage the feat of empathy.

PATRICK shrugs.

[PATRICK] I'll make a stew, then.

the woman on the bathroom floor
cheek, pressed on cold tile and she is frozen,
frozen and unable to twitch a single finger
in her numbness
single eye rolling and blinking the ice from her lashes

the sink is dripping, dripping, like the ticking of a clock
each one like crashing hammer, she is never enough
chill brisk and unrelenting, skin glazed a rosy red
soon the tile cracks, pried open, and out peek those
bulging, terrible eyes, the light flickers out and they're
glowing, glowing a monstrous red, the red of wrong. the
red of paralyzing judgment.

it was a burning as cold as the ends of the earth
and she crawled towards the window, frostbitten
hands outstretched towards the white-

The bear looks down at you and sniffs. Its eyes glow in twilight delusion. You hold your breath. Your lungs are iron red, tight. Swaying mushrooms sprout from its back like crops emerging from freshly tilled earth.

It licks you, and you giggle.

Even My Bones

these thoughts have taken flight in my mind

their ravenous beaks snapping, screeching

bird-songs to claim the voice of God.

flesh turned feather and bone fragile as a twig,

each talon hooked upon a chain bearing cross,

dancing midair bathed in red.

it is a flurry of movement, beady eyes bulbous and

desperate, fear of doubt ever-diving.

it is a splintering crash upon the pavement.

it is chirps twisted into infernal screams.

it is sin as the cross lays between them,

a malicious metal in headlights,

untouched by the blood.

The earbuds in his ears are buzzing,
thrumming and vibrating like bees, on a
beat-beat-beat.
He sniffs, his nose is running.
It's running to Alaska; it heard good things about Alaska.
He wipes his noseless face. He removes his earbuds,
clean and white and corded. A few years old, now, and
the left side isn't quite as loud as the right.
He sticks them in the holes where his nose used to be and
sniffs, inhaling the beats,
and feels his brain dance in the noise.

"Death doesn't suit you," the sailor says, face lined with age so brittle and broken that you could see the lines of wrinkles below his eyes, eyes that raged with the waves of a lifetime, a sea that was settling into calm. At the time I am but a child… of course it does not suit me. Death would fit my frame loose and large, and I would hold my arms up as they drowned in sleeves.

"Death will lay kisses upon your forehead," the priest answered, her warm hands clasped in mine. "One day the angels return to you, to claim that death you owe them. Your blood thickens and your heart beats frantic, fast, until it stops. You cough and tire of fever, of chills, of sores and blisters." It sounded scary. I did not want that day to come. It would not be today, or tomorrow- but it would certainly come, crawling over the rise of suns and moons, over the dull trudge of time.

"Death will save you," the soldier said to me, swollen scars slashed over a face mangled and forgotten. "As it should have saved me, when my friends were bloodied and slain." And I can hear the truth in his voice, the longing that filled his bitter words, and it is the *truth*- but it is not the truth for me.

"Do not torment yourself over death, child," my mother scolded, but it was the sweet kind of scolding, the kind that filled my aching lungs with laughter. "Such things feel foul, from a mouth like yours."

Don't let the seeds see you steal their water.

27

Even My Bones

The leaves are moving. A shimmering tide I see, of faded
green and dark lush together, twinkling like starlight.
They're twitching and fluttering on their branches, blown
astray by the breath of God, high above me in the great
scape of the sky.

And the earth below feels firm, and anchored. I do not
think it would so easily swallow me up, if it tried.
There is something to be said when they tell you to walk
barefoot, to discard your sneakers and press your soles to
the soil. That it grounds you. It is true.
My skin is to the grass, to the dirt, and I feel it- the soul
of the world. I know this is what the natives speak of,
when they whisper their tales of great forest gods and
nature sprits, of mountains that crack their eyes open
between crumbling stone and a sky that speaks in shades
of cloud.

There are birds above, encircling, far out of reach. Their
wings are spread and I think that I would feel wrong like
that, if I lifted my arms and bore my chest open,
vulnerable and bare. I try it on the grass. I try it like the
bird, as if I am the one flying, but I only feel more
tethered to the ground.
That's fine.
I'm more comfortable here, anyway.

Morning train, emerald fluorescents and grooved steel
6am mass of bodies, a swaying sea of suits and
briefcases, faces withered and worn. Shadows hang
heavy under sleepy eyes like raisin bruises and I shiver,
in cold Chicago air.
Do it again, and again.
Morning train. 6am mass. Eyes like bruises.
Go on, again.
Emerald fluorescents, swaying suits.
Again.
Cold air.
Again.

Even My Bones

HA! The jester shrieks, pointing at me. HA! HA!

The court laughs. They are wearing colors I can see and
colors I can't, a myriad of them, like stained glass.
Clothes that shimmer like armor. I shrink away.

HA! HA! HA!

They have heads of doves. Heads of lions, and bears, and
rabbits. Their beady black eyes regard me with humor. A
cicada throws a sour tomato.

HA! HA! HA!

The king is shapeless. He wears a cowboy hat and
several pins on his blazer, but his face is different. His
face is so different that my mind cannot comprehend it.
Were I to describe it, I would say it looked like a
television, broadcasting a thousand channels on the
screen that was on fire.

HA! HA! HA!

Where to go? Where to stay?
My heart aches in this lonely place, this cave I have
squeezed myself deeper and deeper into, crushing
tunnels changing their tunes. These bodies are not *ours*,
they are not on our *side*-
Where to go (if I can go)
Where to stay (if I can stay)
In the dark,
In the dark,
In the dark.

Even My Bones

*Everyone is worried about things, you know. This or
that, you know, and it's hard. And I say, I imagine you
don't want to talk about it. It must be hard. And, you
know, you can see it is. It is hard.*

*We learned about ocean life at school today. For
Biology. I kind of felt jealous, because I'd never seen it
before. The ocean. Like, only in pictures. It looks really
cool, though. I want to go. I will go, one day. Hopefully.*

*The bear hasn't come back, and Dad just told me it was
a trick of the light, but I don't really believe it. I've been
wandering around the edge of the woods, looking for it
after school. The other day, I found an odd mushroom,
stem broken off. I took it back to the house. It's been
glowing at night, softly, like a candle without melting
wax.*

*There's things I worry about, too, sometimes. Can you
come over, later? I want to listen to music with you.
I want to listen to music, one last time.*

my love for you thrums on violin strings,
hum, hum, hum, my darling

violet, suede, suits with ties so tight they cinch against
your throat and leave your skin slightly chaffed
lust and curls and bruises. bruises.

hum, hum, hum, what is money
what is power
what happens when your eyes flicker over to mine in the
dim light, tired, curious, and
STOP.

what happens
when you see?

"you are cruel," the mirror says, distorted and warped
like clouds in a bright sky above- changing and drifting
in the soft breath of my home that awaits.
and when it rains, it rains clear, though I wish it were
blood, sticky and thick and red because I myself am
blood, I am as washed out as the rain, I am resentful.
there are people on the sidewalk with fish-eyes, glossy
and foggy and blank, how I wish
I could rip them from myself
too long have I tempted myself with violence
too long have I tried to feel alive, again
but the world is chaos and I am *CRUEL* and
I am being washed away in rain
I am being taunted with blood
and in this bitterness I will seethe in quiet anger
and wait for the worms to leech me of this pain
and the crows to peck me clean.

as I wander the desert
I pick lilies from my hair, and wither
beneath the eye of the sun
indecisive, indecisive
call to me with a mouth I don't want to kiss
beckon with a language I don't understand
indecisive, indecisive
I reach my tongue out to wet my lips
the lilies have drained all the water
from my skin
my love is different than yours
my love is
indecisive,
indecisive

[Welcome to; YOUR MIND]
Your dreams. Your subconscious. Your void.
What's real, anyway? You don't know. That's okay. We
here at [YOUR MIND] are working hard every day to
make sure that even if you don't know what's real,
whatever you're seeing should be pretty damn close. Oh-
hold on.

(in the distance) Hey! Hey! *Wait*!

screams, static

Even My Bones

Our arms fit firm, or awkward, or cuddly. Maybe the hug
lasts a second too long, but we both don't really mind.
The blankets wrap themselves around my body like they
were made to be there. When I drink water right from the
faucet, or a plastic water bottle, or sip neatly from a glass
with ice and lemon, I know it belongs there, in me, with
me. These flowers were meant for my hair.
This shirt was meant for my skin.
Those books were meant for my shelves, and your words
for my ears, and these songs for my heart.
These bones
were meant
for my body.

Even My Bones

Ribbons 'round my knees,
Ribbons 'round my knees,
Oh, God bless, and tie the rest
These ribbons 'round my knees.

Even My Bones

I am used to the devil.

She lives under my skin, weaved into the marrow of my
bones so tightly that we are one, we are birthed of the
same womb, birthed of lingering nightmares that leave
me trembling in sweat-soaked sheets.
In twilight she breathes my blood and I can feel it boil,
feel my frustration and anger as a blinding red rage, I
want to crush my finger-bones against drywall and bruise
myself beyond recognition, I want to drown myself in
song, in the loud thrum of its vibrations, in nothing and
everything all at once.
She is honest, I'll give her that-
I am surely not to myself.
I wish for the butterflies hanging in my lungs like
clotheslines to shrivel, and the worms in my gut to
burrow deeper. I wish for my blood to curdle like lemon
in milk-tea and my tongue to forever be glued to the roof
of my mouth.
She wears me like a thin skin,
humming, hiding, a monstrous vile thing
I cannot seem to be rid of.

I can feel her,
inside.

they recoiled from him, a veiled fear in their eyes- yes,
there they were, those beastly eyes of golden ichor
how I wish they could see past its gleam

"Don't you wish-"
stumbling, now, furious
"Don't you wish you could see it?"

I could see now they did not wish it
See what? Those gold eyes asked.
See what?
I could not tell them. I could not tell them that the
glimmer was clearing and I knew, now, the answer.

There are three mechanical pencils on my desk.
A dark blue one, for my sketching. An orange one, for
my homework. A green one, as a spare, for when one of
the others eventually, undeniably, is lost.
A fairy takes a liking to the blue. It is as I am attempting
to draw, which is inconvenient, and I tell it so.
You are inconvenient, I say, frowning. I try to swat it
away, like I would a bumblebee (gentle yet stern), but it
remains.
The fairy laughs, it sounds like bells, and gnaws on my
drawing-blue-pencil with sharp little teeth.
I roll my eyes, and reach my had out for the green,
certain it will suffice.

peel away the skin of my cheeks, scalpel poking, precise
let my eyes wander frantically as you peer over me, mask
high and light as bright as the sun lurking behind you,
poking and prodding. Poking and prodding.
make me pretty, I say
as if what I am is a disease
there might not be much you can do,
as I feel hideous beneath myself,
in places you cannot reach.

Even My Bones

Funky tunes, the jazzman shouts, over the music.
Funky tunes!

I nod. It is an agreeable nod, a nice nod. He nods, too,
and we are both nodding at each other, for some amount
of time, I think it was about three minutes.
The music nods all the time.

Are you alone? he asks me, and I think he is a funny
jazzman, with his loud voice and his long hair.
Yes, mister jazzman, I say, *so alone. So, so alone.* Alone
all the time, probably for much longer than the music has
been nodding. I look down. Green and golden glitter is
on his hands. I think it will stay there forever. When he
goes to work, files his taxes. When he holds his newborn,
there will be glitter, on his hands.

I think about those fingers inside me.
He seems to want to, and I am warm, and as long as the
music is nodding it's okay.
Can I take you home? He asks me, and I kiss him. I don't
think I like kissing much, but I like glitter.
He takes me home and for a while I am with the
jazzman, the jazzman is with me, and we are soldiers
under a battlefield of sheets.

Don't have hands?
Want hands? NEW hands?
Do you look down at your fingers, at your shaking and
sweaty palms covered in blood, and realize you've done
something unforgivable? Do you take a second to vomit,
acid burning your nostrils, panting over the sink before
you stumble your way to the front door? Don't look
behind you. If you do, you won't be able to forget.
You'll never forget.
Hands?
New?

Even My Bones

Here are instructions for bone broth.

1. Get bones. Get a lot of bones. I don't know how many you need, but it's better that you have too many, rather than not have enough.

2. Soak them quickly in water and vinegar. This is for cleaning. This is very important. Cleanliness, in general, is important.

3. Pray. Pray, pray.

4. Get a big pot, fill it with water, and make sure you have a lot of time. A few days, at least. You'll need to watch it until the broth is done. Bring the pot to a boil and wait.

5. Is it done yet? No? Keep watching.

6. I said, keep watching.

7. Why are you crying? Why are you crying? Stop it. Stop it right now. You're upsetting the bones. You're- you're-

This has been; cooking.

Even My Bones

Shooting me a wicked smile, fangs drenched in drool,
face painted over and piano playing a miserable tune.
Disturbing. Off-key. That Joel can't hold a candle, to me
Blood stains my fingers and I lick it off, *he* licks it off,
I'm not a monster I'm not a monster I'm not a monster
My child, weeping, tugging at my shirt,
I made it but it's not real
I made it but it's not real
Weeping-
Not real
Not real
Not real

The organ on the plate is not a liver.
It is not a lung, nor a heart.
She didn't know what it was, only that it was on her
plate, and that she was going to eat it.
"I wish I was an organ," her brother says casually,
blonde hair silk like honeyed tart, lips pursed in a pout.
He was upset, it seemed,
that she didn't share the sentiment.
She doesn't respond. She doesn't know how to respond.
The clouds are orange and the candles are midnight,
wind, parsley. The house creaks and the silverware
rattles. When she looks down at her plate,
the organ is gone.
Her brother has stolen it.

You're sick. You're sick, and you can feel it spreading within you, like a thick honey coating around your insides. You're sick, but you feel safe, in the way children feel safe because there is not much to do but lend their fate to a higher, mysterious control. The red glare of the sky is brighter now, apocalypse, rapture, and it's…

It's still.

Nothing moves but the hazy clouds, and the wind that seems to sway the world sideways. The tree is here, and it's always too warm, and there's sweat on your skin. Right now, there's a head growing on the longest and sturdiest branch. It hangs down by thin white strands of hair, like an overripe plum on the verge of souring. You wait for it to fall at any moment, but it doesn't. It regards you with a wide smile. A wide, gummy smile. Honey begins to drip from its lips and pool down its chin, dripping onto dark blue grass.

Your insides churn with distaste.

Even My Bones

I have a brain freeze
limb from limb, bone from bone
(raw, raw)
my brain melts like ice cream
red ice, creamy and foul
twist my neck, crack my skull,
spoon away at my innards and play pretend
I want to turn inside out
lock myself in the freezer
(raw, raw)
bite my tongue
and scare you.

On a small country road there is a car, and a man who drives it. Fields sway and whisper. All is fresh and anew as a spring afternoon, and as he drives he hums and thinks of the warm dinner he will have when he is home.

FLESH, FLESH, FLESH, FLESH

Perhaps that will have to wait, though, he thinks, when his windshield is hit with a mess of feathers. His brakes screech as he stops, and home seems so far away, now. The man's stomach growls. With a sigh, he gets out of the car, twisting the key and shoving it into the pocket of his jeans.

FLESH, FLESH, FLESH

He recoils, as the tide from the shore, rays of sun from the horizon, evil from light. There is disgust on his face, but it fades, quick and fleeting. He takes a step forward. Then another, and another, until he is reaching down with gentle hand and peeling the wing from the road.

FLESH, FLESH

It is bloody and fragile a thing, this sparrow, and he tosses it to the side. It is not a proper grave, not splayed on top of dewed grass, but it is enough. One day the earth will swallow it whole and claim the death it is owed in its thin, rotting, peeling

FLESH.

You are twelve years old.
You're drinking orange juice and eating pancakes coated
in sweet maple syrup. You have school tomorrow, but
that doesn't matter, because right now your brother is
stealing your apple slices from your plate.
Your family is visiting.
Your uncle smells like oil, and no one mentions it
(because he's a mechanic), and you don't understand that
he's going to be dead this time next year. He's really a
nice guy, if you spent a little time with him. It'll be your
last chance. You should give him a hug. You don't.
The smell really bothers you.

Is pain a lesson? Is it a choice? Sometimes it is both, the furry rats behind the dumpster chitter. They watch with beady eyes as you take a drag from your cigarette.

[GOD] Get up. Get up, Patrick.

[PATRICK] I can't.

The lights are out. Were they ever on?

[GOD] You can. It's dark in here, and I can't see anything. You can't see anything. Don't you think that's eventually going to be a problem?

[PATRICK] Eventually. Eventually will bring me a hundred problems. It's better if I can't see them.

[GOD] They're still going to hurt you.

PATRICK doesn't respond.

apples in my calloused hands

basket in an orchard

bring me home to cider fresh and

windowsill windchimes as I sweat, sweat, sweat

and shower far away.

Drink milk, the disembodied voice says. Drink milk.
There is a glass in front of me, now. A clear glass filled
impeccably. Wet and white and drip, drip, dripping from
some unknown source above. I am sitting at a table,
everything is dark, and everything is black.
Except the milk, of course.

Drink, the voice repeats.

The milk waits. It will wait forever, if it has to.
Drink, the voice says, louder this time. I look up to see a
man with a beard holding a sign in front of me.
DRINK MILK, it says. DRINK MILK. DRINK MILK.
The bearded man points at the sign insistently, at the
faded letters that look like they've been peeled off the
side of a carton, big and obvious. *Are you dumb?* His
eyes are saying frantically. *Can't you read?*

Drink, the voice says, and I realize it is coming from
inside me, from under my skin. I reach down and tear the
skin away on my arm, the muscle falls apart like a well-
cooked brisket, tender and ready to melt. When I reach
bone, the voice is louder, and I begin to cry.

CONSUMPTION.

SATISFACTION.

UNEASE?

...

UNEASE?

if there was something (one thing) anything at all
toast in the kettle and spines in the wall
sink my guts in crockpots, make my eyeballs spin,
swirl around the sauces, and cut me 'till I'm thin.
if there was something (one thing)
anything at all
take a drink and tell me
you managed to recall.

She doesn't mind doing dishes.
Even when the blue dish soap coats her palms, when the sponge is squeezed and pressed to rub, rub, rub into the nearest sauce-coated plate or cereal bowl with half-congealed milk at the bottom.
She doesn't mind when the lizard that lives in the pipes crawls its way past the garbage disposal and starts relaying prophecies. *Your husband is going to cheat on you. Your daughter hates your guts. Someday, sitting on the porch knitting a scarf, you will understand that you should have been a teacher instead of a dentist.*
She doesn't mind that either, even if the lizard's manners aren't quite up to her standards.

static

REPORTER: Good morning, [YOUR MIND]! Welcome to your local news station, brought to you by sourdough- easy to buy, easy to bake, easy to rip apart and feed to the growling shadow in your basement. Sourdough. We're better than every other type of bread.

Today, a lawyer in town for a trial was caught vandalizing the grounds of your old high school. Karl Abel, a man of thirty-two, is a prosecutor who was supposed to be attending court today. He was eventually located at 4:27pm with several bottles of brightly colored spray-paint in his hands.

According to those who witnessed his arrest, the man was "clearly disheveled and insane" and "looked like he was possessed." Of course, this would be impossible, since all possessions have to be approved by the local Board of Directors.

Karl had been drawing strange eye symbols all over the brick walls, of varying different sizes and colors. Only one phrase was repeated- WAKE UP. WAKE UP. WHY CAN'T YOU WAKE UP? Disturbing, isn't it? So far, no one has any clue what it means, or why Karl was warning us about it in the first place. Remember, *you're* dead! You can never wake up.

As a reminder, vandalizing private property will result in a severe fine of twenty-four dandelions and the temporary deletion of your social security number.

Lap up the mud-rain.
Lap up the mud-rain (but don't swallow) in a yard you
should but don't remember. Is it gone yet? Is it gone?
Lightning. Spit out the mud as your hair is plastered to
your forehead and your eyelashes blink away the drops-
watch as spit becomes blood but it's black as the night.
Lightning. An endless stream of it from between your
parted,
kissable lips.
Kiss the mud-rain. Lighting. Lap it up.
Lap it up (but don't swallow)

Lonely?
Care about your mortality and the fact that you need
more windshield wiper fluid, even though you don't
know it yet?
Lonely?
Thinking about how your stomach is a bit upset from the
caramel latte you had earlier and how no one, even you,
can remember your name?
Lonely?

Devil is sitting in the pew. Devil is pretty. Devil has his legs crossed, straitens his tie, and reads from the hymn book. Turning frail pages, so frail that the singing, rubbing legs of a cricket would tear them. Humming. Soft, gentle humming. I forget why I'm here, I'm forgetting memories of being the man outside these doors, and the boy who became that man. The church is empty but for him and me, me and him, and a terrifed priest in the corner who's clutching his silver cross necklace and muttering to himself. It is not Sunday. It is not any day. Days don't exist anymore. Devil looks over at me, and I let my mouth fall open, agape, in shock. With gentle fingers he reaches for my tongue, pressing on it, before delving a little deeper. From me he pulls a silver coin, a quarter, and laughs as if it's the funniest thing in the world, this magician's trick.
My tongue tingles where he touched me, like fire.

[PATRICK] Do you love me?

The bed is gentle. Daylight dapples across it like sweet drops of vanilla ice cream onto cone. Tea steams on the nightstand. Is it calm? Is it ever calm enough?

[GOD] Of course I love you.

[PATRICK] But you don't know me.

[GOD] No. I AM you. Always. For all of time. I am everyone. I made you as I made myself, and I love the things I make.

[PATRICK] I'm not sure how I feel about you. I'm not sure if you're really even here at all.

A bird chirps.

Even My Bones

All is frantic and breathless, beneath the sun.

You are sitting at the table, and you are thinking about ice. You are thinking about how it is slippery, like oil, but frozen, unlike oil (most of the time). It is in your glass right now, and you stare at it, as the cubes shift and rise in their bath of lemonade. You lean down and lick gently. You do it again, ice on your tongue, and start lapping at your drink like a dog.

You think about cars. You think about how she hadn't wanted one until she was sixteen, and then that's all she wanted, but who's to know what else a teenager wants? Freedom, like lemonade, was sweet. Also like lemonade, it was sour.

You think about ice, and cars. You think about the fact that one day the two collided and she veered off the road, slammed into a tree, shot through the windshield and impaled herself on a mail post that a neighbor had just finished dismantling because "we haven't gotten any letters in years."

You think about ice. You think about cars. Mostly you think about what you're going to have for dinner tonight.

DRINK
MILK

2

BLOAT

This is… disgusting.
I don't think you would recognize yourself. What's happening to you? I'm sure you're unfamiliar with the process. The insects (I've never been fond of bugs) are burrowing inside you. *What a feast!* They cry, bellies swollen. Bellies, swollen. It looks like you've gained weight, but most of it is gas, and thank the lord you're underground because the smell is atrocious.
Hang in there, buddy.
Hang in there.

Even My Bones

Moonlight and apple crisp, trees laced in silver night-
It is calm in the valley of my dreams.

Even My Bones

My eyes fall out of their sockets with the ease of slipping
through time, bloodshot and slimy and small.
I dip them in cola, fizzy and sweet,
It burns a little because
because there's acid in soda pop,
phosphoric acid, carbonic acid, citric acid.
The label reads them in tiny blocked black letters so
small I would need my glasses to read them, but my
glasses are in the drawer, and my eyes in the soda, and I
cannot see.

Even My Bones

Luck is terrible. Luck doesn't even exist, that's what I think. I also think that I need to switch to a new brand of shampoo and sidewalks need to be an inch wider.

The ocean is beautiful. I wish you could see it. I don't know where you moved to, but you never told me, so I can't even have that. Right now it's cast in the light of explosives and wet with oil- flames dance across its surface and burn it- there's been some awful accident. That's what I mean by luck, by the way. I didn't get hurt. Not even a scratch. Looking at it now, it's weird. It's ugly at first, but then I look past that, the horizon stretching so far our ugliness can't reach it, at the white sun and glittering waves; and I think that it is beautiful.

I don't, like, believe in the astrology stuff. But my horoscope said I'd get lucky today. It kind of makes me mad, but you know, I'm sitting here watching the ocean burn and I'm wondering if the stars are onto something.

She's buried in the couch, sinking into cushions as
brown and deep as the cave systems of America, dotted
across a scatterplot map. Caves are not warm but she is,
under blankets quilted by mom's hands,
sewn in bits of song.
She reads of farm animals, of pigs and cows and
chickens, of hay bales and a sun so bright it makes the
world so much brighter. There's a barn with red chipped
paint and a crosshatch of white, and she's there with
wheat in her mouth and laced boots on her feet.
The animals sing and she joins them-
The birds on the wire, the cow over the moon,
The sheep debating if they should hop the fence.
And she does not worry of how she sounds,
for her brother is with her,
and they sing in wreaked harmony together.

The ghost of her father is sitting beside her.

"You left me alone," She whispers softly, turning slightly to look at him. He hasn't changed a bit. She'd been starting to forget his face, but now that he's here, it was as if nothing had changed.

"We're all alone," he explains, brushing back the loose strands of her hair. "And in death, always."

bless me, breath of newborn foal

baptize me under the sun of a new day,

under a rainbow of light soft on wooden pews

cool water and distant laughs

not a memory. This peace exists only

in imagination.

[PATRICK] I can hear them. I- I can hear angels singing to me. I can hear them!

[GOD] What do they sound like?

PATRICK hesitates, itching his mustache. He wants to say they sound like the flow of golden sunlight, like the sky when it has decided we deserve to see it blue, like the daisies he'd been growing on his windowsill pushing their roots deeper, deeper, deeper into the pot. He says none of this. He does not have the right words, so instead, he makes his best guess.

[PATRICK] They sound like… a choir? Maybe one of them has a guitar. They're good.

GOD bellows his laughter, and it shatters the moment of peace PATRICK had been enjoying. It is such a horrible, incomprehensible sound and he wishes it wouldn't haunt him so, this deity. This nightmare. This god.

He winces, curling in on himself, tears brimming at the corners of his eyes. His hands rise to his ears, pressing, deeper and deeper and deeper into his head.

She is on my lap. She has a skirt that's black and hair that's black and skin, too, that is black. It is nighttime and I feel like I can barely see her, this goddess in the dark, but for the whites of her eyes and teeth. She is a warm, earthy magma seeping over me, burying us under volcanic rock, us girls together. It would take years for it to harden but I would remain under her that long, pleased until geologists cracked my shell and observed me under a microscope. When I reach beneath her skirt, she sighs, and I strengthen my resolve to keep her there.

The pumpkin man offers me syrup.
It's thick and purple and tender as a fresh bruise, as
supple as a grape off the vine, a treat I often crave. My
tongue welcomes it with roaring bells of feast and song,
my sword is raised to the gentle skies, honor and victory.

The pumpkin man makes me pancakes.
There are chocolate chips inside, melting as ice melts on
the eve of springtime, a soft melt, a lovely melt. They are
fluffy, almost proud, and settle in my stomach as
butterflies settle on flowers, one by one.

The pumpkin man brews me coffee.
It is coffee that boils and stews in an earthly slumber,
fumes of forgotten kisses and dreams. Dark, and warm,
searing my lips with that fresh kind of burn.

It is breakfast, and the pumpkin man sits across the table,
tucking a napkin into his neckline.

All of me is saying that I failed. I agonize over our words like there's something hidden inside them.
Not everyone can like you, my feet say. I stare at them as they grow eyes and wriggle like the tentacles of a kraken. My feet say, not everyone is perfect. And you're not perfect. So, there's going to be some unfortunate things that happen, you know. That's how it goes.
I stare at the ceiling that is not the sky.
My feet return to normal.
That's how it goes.

Is it hot? Is it cold? Can you feel anything? Why can't
you feel anything, huh? What's wrong with you? Can we
go to the beach today? Can we go to the beach? Can we-

I am driving at night. It's not a pleasant thing, driving at night, though many people might find it just as unpleasant to drive during the day. I am not one of those people, but I can understand why they feel like that, as I crest the hill and my headlights reach barely further than a few feet away. The radio's static informs me that the next song is a new release, my engine light clicks on, and the yellow lines on the road have tripled in quantity; yellow, yellow, yellow. Am I making you paranoid? Do you have a sense that this is unusual, eerie, unnerving? Are you worried? If not, you should be. We should all be worried, when we're supposed to be.

Especially driving at night.

You are eighteen years old.
You've had a lot of firsts, haven't you? First time in the
grip of a hazy smoky high, first electric kiss, first sip of
lukewarm beer. You don't know if you care for it all that
much. You have big dreams on the horizon, champ. Big
dreams. When you were five you said you wanted to be
an astronaut. Now, the thought of shooting up to the stars
makes you want to throw up.
You find out being a teenager isn't all it's cracked up to
be. You get mad. Your parents become faceless, looming
figures. They haunt you through your cell phone.
You get a tattoo. You get another one.
You apply for college.
When you drink orange juice, this time it's to get rid of
cottonmouth, when you make pancakes it's a rare treat,
and soon you'll leave your brother behind,
and you will have
all your apple slices
to yourself.

I was shaking.

Shaking like a bobblehead on the dash of a car, that was how I felt, distorted and unreal. I'd tossed my childhood away and couldn't find it again, no matter how much I searched with reaching fingers blindly over the floor, in a haze of panic. It was behind a corner, trapped under a floorboard, lost in a vent.

I was shaking.

How could this have happened?

How…

Let them cut you to ribbons,
and float away.

"And you'll be there when I'm born?"
"I'll be there when you die."
"And you'll be there before?"
"And after."
"In sickness?"
"In health."
"Forever?"
"And always."
"Because you love me?"
"Because I love you."

static

REPORTER: Good Morning, [YOUR MIND]!
Welcome to your local, loveable, news station.

Today, in the genre of Kentucky Blues, our local band
The Peeled-Grape Cowboys have brought you three new
songs from their new album.
It was a struggle making ends meet for a while, says lead
singer Bill Thomson, but he's made life-long friends, and
wouldn't give them up for the world. The band tragically
broke up a few months ago when their drummer was
attacked behind the office supply store. After he
recovered from said incident, and learned his lesson
about going places he shouldn't, they decided to turn to
back music for redemption.
What a heartwarming story.

In other news, a six-legged mushroom bear has been
spotted on the outskirts of the Kimmick Farm. It's been
sighted before, but only during blood moons. Some say
that if you lay eyes on it, you'll start going crazy. If there
are any biologists out there, maybe you can figure out
what's causing the drastic change in its hibernation
patterns.

my mother's whispers tether

roots grown in rainy weather

bruised hands are strong,

so play along,

recall her voice together.

my mother's whispers tether

empty everything
in a cell not of stone and bars but of music-
piano, soft and whimsical to play into the very calm and
clouds of a blue sky, insanity
hideous time forgotten and mourned
leave me be, if only.
if only for a while.

Even My Bones

I say, the cow is hungry.
You look at me incredulously. You say, we have never
owned a cow. We have never seen a cow.
What is a cow?
I shake my head, and peer through the old floral curtains
over the sink. You still have dishes to do, but I don't
mention it, because instead I am looking at the field,
and the cow.
I say, I am going to feed it.
I say, internally, why? Why? How?
The cow is looking at me. Its jaw is hanging slack, and
grass falls from its tongue as our eyes try to comprehend
one another. There is hunger there. I am sure of it.
I say, where did we get a cow?
You shake your head and pick up the newspaper.

wake me hazy, scattered yellow
yellow stains of age and withered dandelions stuffed into
the pockets of grandpa's coat, stuffed in the closet,
stuffy nose
cowbell strain and singing frogs
on ships stuck in the waves.

my brother left the couch and
chocolate milk and cartoons
and he never came back.

Even My Bones

There's a red rocket that hangs from my window
In a world where skies are so blue they look like artificial
raspberry slushies, and the clouds are so puffy they could
be fresh marshmallows.
The rocket sways on a string, pretending to blast off
The wind is kind, today.
It creeps through the screen to help.

I don't like to think of you alone out there. In my head, yeah, you're still fifteen. We both are. In my head you, like, still stutter over answers in class and wipe your glasses constantly on your shirt. Like they can never be clean enough.

The bear is real. Remember the bear? That fucking bear I told you about? Maybe I didn't. I don't even remember. Today I went really deep into the woods. Deep, deep- until the trunks of the trees darkened and the earth became muddy. The edges of my new clothes were stained. I had become wild. It was raining, but I was determined. I refused to turn back. I found it sleeping out in the open, beneath a tree bleached completely white. A dead tree, a cursed tree. Its fur was rising as it breathed, and these breaths seemed to seep into the earth, to root themselves, and the mushrooms upon it's back like a shell glowed softly at each pulse of its heart. I didn't want to wake it up, so I left.

Before you moved, you were my best friend. It's been years. Why do I think about you so much? Why do I care? We were kids together. We're not kids, anymore.

So why does it feel like I've lost something?

dark man, dark man
hiding round the door
hiding in the rug, and slinking on the floor
dark man, dark man
break me into bits
scoop me into cereal and eat my steamy grits
dark man, dark man
won't let me creep
kill me first then maybe
I'll find some time to sleep

Even My Bones

rid yourself of silly penance, girl, and kiss
kiss the feet of marble lords
and bite their toes off.

you're standing in the alcohol aisle
the alcohol aisle of the grocery store
music is playing, distant and muted, echoey pop that-
well, it makes you want to run. It scares you.
no one is here. They are other places, not here, never
here. A great green light shines down like a beacon
a beacon in the alcohol aisle.
your mouth begins to dry and shrivel like beef jerky and
you look down at your feet to find them bare, covered in
cuts, swollen as if you'd walked miles but you barely
even remember walking at all.
the green light is cast firmly upon you, alcohol aisle,
grocery store, so you open the door to the breathy, cold
fridge and wrap your hand around the neck of a bottle.

let the willows brush your hair

comb through the tangles and knots

let the lights of the wisps

glass over your eyes

as fireflies gnaw your tongue.

Here are instructions for building a bomb.

1. Whisper to the vents. Whisper that you're angry, that you're resentful, that you have become a pawn in the machine of reckless violence.

2. Open the vents and reach inside. You will find a bag of supplies. Take the bag, and these instructions, over to your workbench.

3. Let your hands move. Twist, screw. Yes. Connect the wires right there. You got it.

4. Step away. Wipe your brow and put your hands on your hips, nodding, satisfied, by the job you have completed. What will you do with it? I hope nothing too dangerous. I hope you will be responsible.

5. Hide it, but make sure to whisper your thanks to the vents before you do. You should always show appreciation when someone helps you out.

This has been; crafts.

The VOID shakes your hand.
It is cold, and also hot, and it takes another second of
indecisiveness before it pulls away and you don't
remember the sensation well enough to make a decision.
It is talking to you (or something like talking) and you
get the sense that the VOID is happy to see you. It
doesn't have eyes, though. But you assume it *can* see
you. You wish it couldn't.
You didn't style your hair this morning.

Even My Bones

Do you love me? The human asks, eyes like moon-
saucers and bags just as heavy beneath them. Wild curls
of hair, unwashed.

I cannot love, the other responds. I am incapable of it.

Are you sure?

The other turns away. He is savage, sorrow, and his
name is DEATH. It is the end of days and there is no
love, it has been so long since he has seen it. Fancy
dinners and red-sparrow wine, mocking laughter of
clowns with two faces. Amusement. Endless visions
beyond the earth. The other chuckles without feeling and
brings him closer, savoring. A kiss is placed upon his
forehead.

Can you love *me*? The human asks again.
As if this is different.

The other taps one sleek shoe against the tile, thinking.
The water outside splashes cherry against the cliffside.
Yes, he says.
I could love *you*.

Even My Bones

wave to your mother, with your worn finger-bones

harrowed skull caving in on a lonely beach

beach of the will that sucks you in

walk, walk towards the grey sea

and leave us behind.

static

REPORTER: Good Morning, [YOUR MIND]! Welcome to your local news station- and boy, do I have news for you!

Last evening, members from the cult of *The Sacred Iris* were caught stealing radio equipment, batteries, and ring pops from the gas station on Pillbox Avenue. The five culprits were all wearing masks made of leather, with goggles sewn in. I'm not sure how they were able to see anything, given that the goggles were marked up with spray paint, but they said that "the spirits of the *Eyes* guide our way." Not sure how useful that is, considering that they knocked over several shelves during their robbery, but to each his own.

The cultists insisted they were trying to get a message to someone- they want you to WAKE UP. WAKE UP. YOU CAN'T GO YET, YOU'RE NOT READY. YOU'RE NOT READY. I'm not sure what that's all about, but I hope they were able to find whoever needed to hear it.

The perpetrators are being held at Winsor County Jail. Their mothers are very upset.

[GOD] I am here to forgive you for sin.

[PATRICK] But what if I cannot forgive myself?

The field is open. PATRICK fists his hands into the dirt, digging his own grave, but the frozen soil won't let him. It is too hard, and his hands are too numb. Blue, at the fingertips.

[GOD] It does not matter. You are forgiven.

PATRICK is crying softly. His tears are of ice. His lashes flutter with snow.

[PATRICK] I don't deserve it.

[GOD] No. I don't suppose you do.

lay back in bliss, in scratchy grass with blues skies
watch the clouds climb up and up, around
sun beams and picnic smiles
wait for the trees to pick you up in withered arms and
carry you, carry you into their mouths of bark and seeds,
strands of hair in branches. How they feed on you, roots
through a coffin, rooting you to the earth.

"ah, my sweet,"
she gurgles with orange-tinted teeth
and eyes that slant like they're melting
she doesn't touch me, doesn't need to
only stands on the street corner
the traffic lights flash in warning.
"ah, my sweet,"
and brings her fingernails up to bite.
"Mom," I say, stepping forward. "Mom."
she is a goldfish. She swims to me, around me,
analyzing.
"Mom, mom, mom!" a mantra. A song.
she doesn't recognize me
cannot tell me apart
from the baby
in my petal pink photo albums.

the cat has red heads today.
thunder struck in Kansas,
and my gems shine under the man on the moon.

The tree is weak.
It weakens with each blow you deal to its base. For some
reason, the axe feels heavy in your calloused hands,
heavier with each swing you land. The wood has
splintered away and the organs are in full view,
pulsating, overflowing.
What will it take to make them stop? Nausea builds as
you watch the scene, bloody and rancid and infectious.
What will it take to make them go away?
You'd feel better with them gone. With this tree,
looming and rotting, out of your sight. You can't seem to
leave it, you can't seem to walk away.
The mass of leaves growl above you, a terrible wet,
guttural squeal, and when you turn to look up,
they've wilted to brown.

cell towers across the plains, spanning far

headlights of lone, rusted cars

blood of the lamb crushed under hooves

hooves of your grinning, guilty hymn

steel and wire, smoke and fog

sin for the earth and let it call your name

bitter fruit of will and shame.

"Is this pain worth it?" I scream, stumbling. "Is it worth
it? Please, please! I must know!"
It must lead to something. It must
have a meaning meaning meaning
Do you see the hill on the horizon? The trees that gather
for you? The way their organs pulse and beat under their
bark, their life, their spark of nerves that makes their
leaves flutter. It must
be a meaning meaning meaning
the pain.
It must be…
a meaning, meaningful
pain.

Even My Bones

Cascading. Do you think-
Sunlight, unstoppable, the way it smiles down (has
smiled down) your whole life, in a daycare center
painted over a rainbow, on well-wishing cards and
always, always above.
Do you think? Do you think of that?
Don't think too hard, because the sun is getting closer,
smiling wider and wider with molten rows of teeth like
cards being set neatly in a row in front of you, one two
one two, red or blue? Red or blue? It has eyes that you
can't see and a tongue that masses like rising yeast,
lolling from between cards, licking light onto your skin.
Do you think?
Think again.

dark screen, dark and mean, dark and-
oh lord, don't scream
simmering over and under your eyes
strained and unable to be pried open, no
dark loathing, tripping hard, high
ice baths and soaked joints
don't scream
lord, please don't scream.

Break open the soda can
and speak to the beetle that drowns inside.
"The sun!" it screams, hissing, trying to back away into
the broken sanctuary that was now spilling carbonated
sugar over the concrete. "The sun!"
The sun smirks its indifference, burning.
"Yes, yes," you say, waving your hand. "But why am I
here? I must know why I am here!"
The beetle screams acid and radio static.
I look up at the sun.
It shrugs, and I
cannot bear to look any longer.

You're running.
Run faster.
There's a stitch in your side just like there was in middle
school when the gym teacher made you run the mile.
Only difference is that this time you can't stop.

There's something in the fog behind you.
It's swirling, and misty, and smells like a slightly
familiar but unplaceable cologne. Keep your pace.
You're stumbling. You've tripped. Your ankle is broken.

Run.
Run faster.
The pain in your ankle is nothing compared to what's
hiding in that fog. Your lungs are contracting, limbs
seizing and flailing wildly in panic; gasping,
hyperventilating, slowing down. Slowing down.

You trip again.
You don't get back up.

the bane of what we make, all gone up in smoke
my terror is fragile, and you dread when you awoke
drip-drop into panic and
you splatter and you spread
you're all over it like jelly
on my toasted crunchy bread.

This journal is falling apart. It's been, what, ten years now? I sat in my foreign history class today, thinking about the debt racking up under my name, sad, like always, tired, like always, lost, like always. We watched a documentary.

It's hard not to be disheartened, watching shit like that. The battlefield is paper men who bleed too easy. They found a man dead in his cot. He'd vomited all over the front of his uniform, and the rats had started to eat his flesh away. In the trenches, they had nowhere to bury him. Not until the fire died down. The boys were not boys anymore- someone has scrunched and molded their faces into wrinkled old men. Their mothers would not recognize them.

I think they had to grow up too fast. I think I was already growing fast enough, and here they were, going super-sonic; growing greys at the ripe age of eighteen.

I wondered if their bones were still out there somewhere, rolling miserably in their graves.

bathe me in your misty tears, for I love you
red and bright as the magma-blood of the earth, boiling
over and consuming, knowing, pinpricked flesh
sharp teeth sinking deeper and deeper until we cannot
separate, I cannot tear you out, thorn, thorn, thorn
I hate you, oh, yet yearn for your
hands on my head, gentle, fond, and
guiding.

Do you hear that? It's just me? Why is it always just me? Are your ears frozen from where your head is buried in the snow? Is it snowing, or are you on fire? Can you tell? How? Can you ever trust your nerves or ears or eyes or blood or bones?

"You're a doctor," I say, in a doctor's office, in a hospital, in front of a man wearing a white coat and holding a clipboard as a certification that yes, surely, he's a doctor. My palms sweat to warn me I am anxious, that I'm uncomfortable, but I clench them in my shirt because now is not the time. I don't like the feeling of sweaty palms. It would probably be hard to find someone who does.

The doctor smiles with a smile that's meant to be comforting, but it can't be, since there's a dark fleck stuck in his teeth. "Let's take a look at those X-rays," he says. "Let's take a look under all that flesh."

I tremble. Rather, it is not me that trembles, but something beneath. I don't want to think about it. I *can't* think about it, because my attention is still set on the fleck of black, perhaps pepper, between his flashing teeth. What did he eat for lunch? How long ago? Did anyone even bother to tell him- and if they did, did they watch as he picked and picked and picked and failed, smiling and nodding when he'd asked if he'd gotten it?

My gaze is drawn away when he pulls up the X-rays. The tremble inside me grows to a persistent itching. Green light bathes the images of my bones, and I know, then, that something is wrong. Misshapen, deranged. And it is upsetting. It is so, so upsetting.

"Something's wrong." Terror alters my voice.

"Seems healthy to me."

I shake my head. "No, no. That's not right."

"It is right. I'm a doctor, right?"

"Right?"

"Right."

The fleck in his teeth makes his smile a lie, so I turn on my heel and run out the door.

the wounded in the chapel,
practice perfect prayers
and don't let those filthy sinners
grab your oiled hands

In the library, there are books, but there are also more than books. Outside the windows there is, as usual, void- a purple sky, and sand, sand that makes up a desert, stars that twinkle above. Maybe it is endless, maybe it is nothing, but here, in this library, it ends. And it is something.

I sort through the shelves aimlessly, I know I am looking for something, something important, but the titles blur against my eyes as if I am not meant to read them. A giant RAT scuttles up to me, skin sagging, as if he is not a RAT but something hiding in the suit of one.
He tells me about a show, tomorrow. He tries to sell me tickets, waves them in front of me. They glitter gold. Tickets, he says. Tickets for the show.

I shake my head and turn back to the books. I am not here for a show, I am here for whatever is written in these pages, surely it will be visible to me, when I come upon it.
Tickets! RAT says, throwing them around. Tickets to the show! Tickets to the show! Please! *Please*!
The purple sky outside, and the sand below it, and the void that is everything, remains unchanged.

You are twenty years old.
You're scared.
You're always scared, now, even though you're an adult
and it's been a long time since you hid under your covers
from the monster in your closet. Time is moving too fast,
and you're not changing at all. College doesn't pay, and
you haven't eaten pancakes in forever. It is hard.
You expected it to be, but not like this.
You make mistakes, and that's okay. Usually it's cold,
and usually you have a jacket, and usually there's
homework.
One day, your car breaks down and you smell something
familiar and wrinkle your nose. You remember your
uncle. You watch the oil pool under the tires and stand
there for a very long time.

The angel sets down their guitar. They're draped in a simple robe, wet hair dripping in curls around their shoulders. Strange eyes meet your own and they are filled with galaxies, nebulas, a light you are not yet allowed to touch. White wings flutter, soft and ethereal.

"Did you like it?" They ask. "Wrote it myself."

"You did?"

The angel nods.

"It was lovely."

"You really think so?"

You hum your approval, and the angel grins.

bitter kisses, staining my tongue, magic
I've been here with you before, can't recall when
sobs swelling in my throat.
you've stolen my heart, haven't you?
what a lover, but you won't give it back.
you won't
give it
back.

Even My Bones

There is a zipper
That trails from my sternum to my pelvis
It was not there before, in the before I remember, but it is
here now- and like
my morning coffee, violence on the news,
the constant dull trudge of a never-ending workday,
and winter, laundry, emails-
I got used to it.

It was a firm, perhaps fearful decision, that I did not dare
to unzip it. What would be inside?
Did I want to know?
Sometimes I traced the path of it in the mirror, cold
ridged metal on my fingertips, an access to... inside.

In the now that was after the before,
A bear found me as I slept and did what I could not-
It took the zipper in its teeth and pulled down, loud and
grating in the stillness. I watched in horror as it began to
eat, maw deep in my torso, muzzle covered in honey
when it retracted.
"Are you sick?" It asked. Its voice was the sound of
splintering wood. Crack. Crack. Crack.
"Are you sick?"

I MEAN,

IT HURTS.

IT'S ALWAYS GOING TO HURT

AND THAT'S OKAY

Even My Bones

carry me static, burdened, lost

six feet down and pay the cost

corpse soaked in waters, cradles thin

brittle, overturning brim

what I cannot comprehend
evades me, insight, moonlight, out and in
you're crazy you're crazy you're crazy and I
cannot lie cannot lie cannot lie cannot lie cannot lie

Even My Bones

Long was the day that has passed, somehow forgotten.
Already it has blended with those that came before.
The bathroom is the end of it, the bathroom is separate,
far away from such days that dreg on.

I can barely even feel the spray, it is nothing like rain,
It is warm, and enveloping.
It surrounds my body in a fog, this body that is not my
own-
I am separate, distant, a fleeting thing.
I don't know if this body is anyone's, but it surely isn't
mine. My eyes are closed, closed against the onslaught,
and I see a light. I see it past me, out of reach, a light
beyond waking shores, a light shaped like a door and
through that door is something my mind tries to fill but
cannot. Not even words, thoughts, a wisping breath could
conceive of it.
And when I falter, when my eyes flutter awake, despair
floods the corners of my vision, and the door is gone. It
is gone and can only be found in lonely bathroom nights
when the rest of the world does not exist.

I am sitting on the floor of the shower, and I must get up.
How it pains me to leave it behind,
and face the days I still have ahead.

3

ACTIVE DECAY

Wow. Yikes.
You've lost a lot of weight (ha). Most of it is gone. Most
of it is mush, your internal organs and various tissues
resembling a smoothie. Certainly not a smoothie
someone should drink, but you get the idea. We're
getting down to the good stuff. You might have been
fond of your skin, of your flesh, but you can say your
goodbyes. Take your time- you have a lot of it.
That mole on your shoulder? That scar on your heel?
That strange rash in the pits of your elbows? Yup.
Everything you used to be is disappearing.

Maybe it's already gone.

peaches are yellowed and fuzzed,

while twitches roam tunnels in toes

and all that is nothing is yours, my love,

for aspens will grow from your bones.

Even My Bones

There is blood in places there hasn't been blood before.
Dark blood, thick blood, watered-down blood that looks
fake, movie set, strawberries. There are wild strawberries
out back in the yard, under sun and moon they grow
from sour white to flush and full. My flesh is blood, in
the shower it drips, drips down to my painted toes and
lightens my head. The strawberries are sweet, when I
want them to be. The strawberries are not always where
strawberries are. Sometimes, they are somewhere else.
Thick, watered-down. Are you scared? I am scared.
Scared of blood, and fruit, when I cannot pick it from the
earth. It is not a gift it wants to give me.

"Mister Shadow," the girl whispers, clutching her covers
to her chin. She is peering over them like they are the
precipice of a jutting cliff spanning off into darkness.
"Are you alive?"
The hallway light is on.
A shadow stands in front of it,
earning his well-suited name.
He does not respond.
Elsewhere, the kitchen sink drips at an even interval, and
an indistinguishable bird lands on the telephone wire
outside; it pecks the wire open, exposing its innards as a
feast of copper, and promptly electrocutes itself.
"Mister Shadow, are you alive?"
Are you alive?
Are you alive?
The bird outside is not.

the TV's black and static
your fish-eyes droop to sleep
I hate the way I feel at night
my thoughts dig graves too deep.

Even My Bones

In my car there is a carton of mints. Arctic mints that are
green, milky green, green that has been tampered with. It
still feels strong in my mouth, like carbonation, ice
water. Like when you lick snow fresh and fallen.
The car door opens.
I am annoyed. I am here, he should not be. I am my
music and my peace, I am myself, and he is a stranger.
And that was sickening.
And I said, Man, get out. Get out of here.
He turns to look at me with one eye. It is glowing, and
green. Endless scrutiny and tears as thick as lotion. No,
wait, he isn't crying at all. He only stares.
Man, I said. What do you want? Man? Man?
With trembling, frostbitten fingers I open the tin. Mints
rattle around in there like pills in a bottle, rattle rattle.
I offer the Man a single mint.
He takes it, plucks it from my palm like a mother bird
plucks a worm from wet soil,
even though he doesn't have a mouth.
He does get out of my car, though.

this little girl is scared
because the world is starting to peel back its skin
peeling it back like an orange
you didn't know was too ripe
it spills its guts over her fingers in citrus decay
my mother assures me.
she assures me that it will be alright.
how hollow it feels.
I have missed so much.

You are thirty years old.
You open the door to your apartment and find it empty,
lights off. Alone. You sigh, set your keys on the counter,
and dread over the thought of making dinner.
The collar of your work shirt itches. When you open the
fridge, casting a blue light across the tile, you spot the
last few drops of orange juice and bring the bottle to your
lips. For some reason, it doesn't taste the same anymore.
Tired, you call your Mom. "Hey, Mom."
"Hey. Why are you calling?"
"I don't remember. I miss you and I love you and I just
want to play with those blocks again, you know? The
yellows and greens and blues. There was even a red
one."
"I don't know what you're talking about," she says.
But she does. And you do, too.
And you never speak of it again.

Break dance. Dance, dance, break. Break. Break.
Break your limbs. Snap them. Take a hold on your arm,
and wedge it between the gaps of that chair. Now, twist.
Twist hard. Put all of your weight down on it. Pant. Pant
heavily and groan, let it fall limp at your side. Go get a
drink at the bar- a sweet one. With cherries. The music is
playing and you need to dance. Break dance. Dance.
Dance.

I do wonder what you're up to, nowadays. I stayed here in our little town- maybe because it's safe, or because I'm weak, or because maybe I think I might see that bear again. It's the only interesting thing that's ever happened to me and I'm too scared to walk away.

I talk to you in this journal because there's no one else. In my head you're still seven, or nine, or twelve (we both are), and we're lying on the carpet spilling all our childish secrets.

I don't know what to do with myself. Sometimes I'm pulled in a million directions, and sometimes nowhere at all, and the clock keeps on ticking. I took myself out, today. On a walk in the woods. If I ran into the bear, which I didn't, I would have let it claw right through me like I was paper. Paper that bleeds way too easy.

I would have let it devour me whole.

static

REPORTER: Good morning, [YOUR MIND]!
Welcome to your local news station. Recently, we've
been getting complaints about the organ shortages lately.
Fake news might try to tell you it's all because of the
plague going around, but I assure you, it's nothing like
that. Don't listen to the government. Don't listen to
anyone. Lock yourself in a bunker with a hundred guns
and endless cans of beans.

Meat is necessary for the human diet. Meat, eat meat. Eat
meat all the time and grow big and strong. This message
is sponsored by… uh, there seems to be a typo here. It
just says something demonic looking in Latin.

Organs, when sold, are never labeled as to tell us what
they actually are. It's better not knowing, the cashiers
say, hiding their wince behind a classic customer-service
smile. Don't antagonize them, and don't pay with cash.

In the meantime, fulfill your organ needs by going
fishing with your Pops. He'll tell you that he's not a
fisherman, because that's an embarrassing thing to be
nowadays with the whole scandal going on, but he is. All
Dads are secretly fishermen- so grab your explosives and
your homemade toffee and get on out there!

Maybe don't go today, though. There's a lightning storm
expected this evening and the fish will be hiding, utterly
afraid, under the mud.

Even My Bones

When you hold the strawberries to my lips
I tangle my fingers in the vines under my knees,
preparing, grounding myself into the soil where they
were grown.
Under the bushes, we are away from the world, we are as
tiny and small as the caterpillars that inch their way
across the leaves. Sunlight manages to embrace me- to
touch my skin, even way down here. Hidden.
"Why are you trying?" I ask, laying my head down with
a sigh. "Why are you trying to reach me?"
The sun pulses, and I know it is saying it's because I am
sweet, and it wants to watch me grow.

I want to be a son to my father
Laughing over things we both understand
The things
men
understand

I want him to buy me a drink on my twenty-first
birthday-
of course, it wouldn't be my first
but I would want to pretend that it was.

I want to
go back to when things between us were easier
When I could ride on his shoulders and grab his hair
As I grow up our differences grow too, we cannot help it,
I have become something else to him, something strange
and far away, that's what womanhood is, isn't it?
I am one brain and he is another, in separate tanks
floating like preserves, labeled as individuals
because that
that is what I have finally become.

I want to be a son to my father
Laughing over things we both understand
the things men understand
I just
don't know
if I can.

my heart is beating out of my chest
out of my chest, it's breaking my bones,
squeezing itself through my ribs like a
crushed gusher candy
oozing out of myself
rapid, frantic beats
painful
I didn't know it could be painful
I felt hazy and weird and scared, trying to grasp onto the
strings of my own body but I was losing them like the
strings of balloons slipping through my fingers.
breathing was a thing of fantasy
I had to take my lungs and press them in and out, make
them move, *force* them to move,
because they had forgotten.
humiliation dug deep into my gut like roots into the
tresses of the earth, yes, but I couldn't linger
on its cruelty.

even my bones cry
it is not a crying with tears
it is a different kind of crying. I can't do it with my eyes
but that sort of thing
has to go somewhere.

Something whispers to me, in the dead of night. It is so dead that even my clock is asleep, I have no way to tell the time, but for the moon that hangs heavy in the sky through my bedroom window. Its whispers are so close to me, but I cannot tell where they are coming from, only that I must listen.

I emerge from my sheets and bare myself to the moonlight, how pale I look, how vulnerable. Is that really what I look like? I make my way to the kitchen and find it emptier than I am used to, darker, more fragile. The tile is cold. The moon is cold. It is bright tonight. I open the fridge and am encased in a vibrant blue light, and reach for the milk carton. Before I realize what I am doing, the rim is to my lips, and the cap is on the floor.

I drink. I am drinking. Drinking, drinking, until my stomach is full and it starts leaking from my nostrils, the corners of my eyes, even my ears. White, dripping down my body. Still, I drink. I cannot stop. Whatever this is, I cannot stop, and the voice urges me on.

I drink until the carton is gone, and I lay on the tile feeling as dead as the night is right now, and the voice has vanished, departed from my memory like a terrible dream.

Are clouds wind? Are clouds water? Do the clouds tell you that a B isn't good enough on your math test, do they whisper secrets no one else will tell you?

"You're alone," the fireflies whisper, buzzing.

One of them settles on a leaf, wings opening and closing slowly, as if stretching. The green light peeks from between the curtains. It's a soft glow.

"No, I'm not," she argues. She tries to think of all the people she talks to, scrambling to defend herself.

"You are," they say, so certain, as if it is a fact. A secret truth.

She frowns, and paces back and forth. "I'm not lonely."

One of the fireflies lands in her hand, snuggling up into her palm, perhaps savoring the warmth.

"That's the point," they say. "Forgetting you're alone."

She lets the bug climb onto the edge of her finger, legs tickling, firmly aware that she is the god in this scenario, and blows it away into the night.

my brother and I shared a childhood
if time is constant, and ongoing (always)
then somewhere we are still
rolling in grass and arguing
begging for candy with clasped hands, our stomachs
could hold so much more sugar, loved with crooked teeth
he is still shorter than me
somewhere we are still
children.

The bear looks down at you with a huff. Your organs drown in blood and milk. The mushrooms look at you with eyes they did not previously have, watching you descend. Its claw rests on your chest, heavy, crushing, and it is a reminder. It is a reminder that you cannot be here forever.

The bear nuzzles your neck, and you sigh.

The bottle dangled from his hand, hanging loosely over the arm of the couch. It wasn't beer, it wasn't wine, wasn't any alcohol that would burn its way down his throat. No. It had taken his father, but it wouldn't take him.

It was a cola, a soda, fizzy and too sweet. Sweet as the air that blew through the curtains- today, it was a breeze rich with the promise of rain. The sidewalk was quiet, all was quiet under the weight of the sky. Things felt distant here. Smoke rose from pillars in the distance, a cat dashed out of the neighbor's shrubbery, and the windchime above the sink rattled its rainbow colors.

There was a pumpkin sitting on the chair across from him, orange and picked right from the patch- or at least, he assumed it had been. Eyes had been carved into its flesh, a haphazard mouth with pointed teeth.

"You want some?" He asked it, holding the root beer out. It sloshed over the tip, foam spilling over the rim.

The pumpkin did not answer.

"Shame," he said, leaning back in the chair. "Don't think I can finish it myself."

Life is so funny. Luck, too, is funny. I know I don't really believe in that sort of thing, but if I did, I would say that mine finally ran out. Whatever fuel was keeping me alive? The gas tank's empty, captain. It's gone.

Sometimes, I think I see it, at the edges of my vision. That bear covered in mushrooms and fur, a bulking shadow with two unblinking eyes. Passing through my hallways. Hiding, just out of sight. Maybe I am finally going crazy.

It's dark here. It's dark, in my head. And I know, in this house, I know in this cage, it's trapping me. What do I do? What do I do, when I don't want to wake up anymore?
What does anyone do?

Bleach burned her nose, as she scrubbed.
It reddened her hands, chemical and strong. A bottle of it
sat beside her as she worked, sweat beading her brow
and soaking her t-shirt. Someone was playing music
outside, hard beats that surely shook the car they were in,
deafening…
from here it was like listening through layers.
She tried to steady her heartbeat,
breaths matching the rhythm of the song,
lungs expanding and contracting with the force
of every fiber in her being.

the living room carpet is covered in blood.
flies buzz in the sunlight, dappling through the window
in a haze of yellow, dim and faded.
windchimes sing through the open door, swinging on its
hinges, creaking.
wheat fields sway in endless monotony past the
farmhouse,
perhaps there is a road buried somewhere beneath them,
but it is out of sight.

There are things you regret.
Words, evil words that you cannot shove down your throat and back into whatever pit you dragged them from. Kind words you didn't mean. Awkward words that settle wrong, like a too-small sheet for a king size bed, and whenever you try to fix it one side keeps popping back up from under the mattress. Well-meaning words that got sorted wrong and they…
They didn't respond how you thought they would.
"I don't know what to say," you respond.
"I didn't mean it like that."
"I'm not good at this sort of thing,"
and you gesture vaguely with one hand, because they know what you are talking about,
and they know what you mean.

Drink milk, the carton says. The store is nearly empty, and you feel empty, and most things, today, are empty.

Huh. Drink milk?

You have never liked milk. Why start now?

But the carton is menacing. It has bold, red letters and they are starting to appear on every label in the store, on chip bags and fresh produce and organ packages. DRINK MILK, it says. DRINK MILK.

Should you listen? Something under your flesh is thrumming like a plucked string of a violin. It is thrumming eagerly. It is thrumming hard.

You admit defeat, throw the carton into your basket, and everything returns to normal.

I don't know my lines.
"That's not your role," the RAT above me says, nose
turned down, looming and pink with flopping whiskers.
"You're doing it all wrong."
I'm doing it wrong. I don't know my lines.
"That's not your role," the RAT repeats,
and I think it looks like a costume,
his grey tattered fur, stained in cola and matted and fake.
There is a face behind those beady black eyes
Many faces, many frowns
Because I'm doing it wrong
but I
don't know
my lines.

PATRICK is dancing. He is dancing alone with no one to watch him but the stuffed bear that's sitting on the counter. He wears pajamas too big for him. The bear still has a tag on it.

[GOD] I like your bear. And your music. Is it for anyone?

[PATRICK] The bear?

GOD nods.

[PATRICK] It's for me.

[GOD] It's a nice bear.

Pause.

[PATRICK] You can have it. I'll get another.

[GOD] That's okay. I don't need a stuffed animal to sleep. In fact, I don't think I ever sleep. I don't even know what sleep is. I couldn't relate.

[PATRICK] But you're *me*, remember?

Irrefutable logic.
GOD takes the bear.

The storm was growing but I could not hear it, it was far away, a distant thing, and my heart had settled my blacked coal between my ribs.

At the coffee shop I work at, we have regulars. Old regulars, new regulars, customers that blend together into one hazy monster of changing faces. All of them want coffee. Of course, I think. This is where people come when they want that sort of thing. It is 7am. I am pouring foam into a latte- it looks like a perfect replica of the *RMS Carpathia*- floating on a sea of espresso and hot milk. I carry it to the counter and call out a name I have already forgotten, eyeing a regular in the corner. She always sits in that same seat every weekend. Unprompted, I begin making her order; an iced vanilla coffee with eight sugars, two sugars, more sugar. It's all sugar, really. It's just a cup of sugar. When I hand it to her, I do it hastily, because the ice is burning my hand and, otherwise, I don't really want to be holding it. She thanks me. The customer-service ghost inside me grabs the edges of my mouth and pulls them into a smile.

Sand and ash in his boots, along a road, a crumbling city road under dunes. Parched throat, dry tongue. Bits of space-rock fell from the sky like confetti, and a dog padded up beside him, panting in the heat.

"Come on," the man said. "Before nightfall."

static

REPORTER: Good morning, [YOUR MIND]! Welcome to your local news station. It's looking chilly out there today, so make sure to stay inside with a mug of hot coco- and if you make a snowman, double-check that you're properly armed beforehand.

This evening, local park ranger Patrick Mallard is alone in an empty field just outside of town. Our source says that he is trying desperately to dig a hole of some sort, and is talking to himself in despair, waving his hands frantically at the snowy, wind-swept grey of the sky. It is cold, our source says, shivering, and the ice is particularly icy today. Acting so existential might be normal behavior for accountants, but Patrick is not, and he's also a nice guy.
I sure hope he's okay.

Have you tried the new Candy-Berry Soda? Well, do I have news for you. It's 50% off for the month of November in honor of Veteran's Day! Thank you, veterans. Those aliens won't be causing us trouble anytime soon.

You are forty-two years old.
You met someone (anyone) and they are nice. Very nice.
They sleep with you and cook with you and smile with
you, and that's all you can really ask of anyone.
Today there is a baby.
Baby, baby, you say. It giggles and grabs your finger.
Something like panic grabs your gut- warm and strange
and terrible and beautiful. You call your Mom.
"Mom, I don't know what I'm going to do."
You remember she's dead now.
The sun is large. The sun is so, so very large.
You set the phone down.

Even My Bones

salt and brine,

salt and brine,

build a willowed, hollow shrine

cast my tears in moon and shine

salt and brine,

salt and brine,

heed me as I long and pine

sip my watered, lemon wine

all is mine

all is mine.

My bike shorts are scuffed, on a red diner chair, summer sign above my head, advertising sweets. The air conditioning tingles my bones. I look down at the milkshake, and the milkshake looks back up at me, with eyes that don't look like eyes, more like cherries, but they're there, and they're looking.

What do you want? I find myself asking, whispering into the cup. Ah, ah, what do you want?

And the eyes roll and a mouth forms out of whipped cream and tries to speak, but there is only a desperate gurgle. The vanilla spits up and gets on my nose.

When I wipe the reside away with my napkin, I lean closer. Closer, closer. Ah, ah, I say. What do you want?

It gurgles some more, and I shrug, unable to understand. I pick up my spoon and dive in. Ah ah, I say, as the cherries roll in terror and the whipped cream shies away.

Ah, ah ah, ah ah.

nimble fingers slide out, long
grotesquely long, from the tomato-soup can in the
pantry. long fingers.
very, very. yes. long.

Even My Bones

My mind is driven wild with this… thing. The bear, I used to think. Now I call it a monster. I don't know what is real, and what's not. For all I know, it hasn't moved from its spot beneath the tree since that night of the blood moon. It could just be haunting my dreams. But I know it's real- I still have it, that mushroom. It's shriveled and old, but I have it.

In my dreams, there are hundreds of them. Mushrooms, enchanting, magical. I feel as if I am walking a dream- as if these are not mine to have. In the dark, they glow, and bathed in heavy light they pale to almost opaque. Thin, and dead. Full, and alive. I walk among them and they whisper things to me, things I can't remember in the morning, and the loss feels like a weight buried in my guts.

I work, I know. I have a job, I know, because I come home every day with a thin sheen of sweat on my skin and a briefcase in my hand. Dressed professionally. I must work, I know, but I don't. I don't know.
Not really.

the piano laughed,
blood gushed into lapping tongues,
and the sun slumped down to sleep.

"I am lonely," she whispered, leaning her head onto the bark. It bit into her scalp unpleasantly, and syrupy sap wept its way down across her neck.

The tree loomed over her, like a mother over a cradle. "I am here. You are not alone."

"Look at me," she argued. The pine needles ticked her bare feet, the wind gusting across the lake. "Look at me!"

The tree looked.

"You see?"

No one can ever see.

"You see?"

The tree wept.

I am filled with a rage
a rage I cannot place
a rage unfit for my position
it is unjustified and irrational in its waves
cascading on a great ocean
no aim but where the wind decides to take it
but wind changes often
and I'm afraid I do, too.

You sit panting beneath a red sky with no sun. The warmth has become soothing, rather than overbearing, and the feeling of your skin melting away was almost a relief. The tree is almost dead. You've almost won. You look at the axe, knowing it weighs at least ten times what it did before you started, the blade gleaming wickedly at you. Your tongue is dry. The smell of sweet golden honey lingers, ever so slightly, in the breeze. You have to battle for your happiness- you have to *fight-* and every glorifying chop is another step closer to the end. In front of where you sit in the grass, the tree groans, and the sound of it echoes across the valley, somehow an inspiration to your befuddled mind. You pick up your axe.

don't heed the tears of others,
that salt will dry your mouth.
your teeth will rot and fall,
if you burden it yourself.

we were very homesick, but also very merry
in thick woods we were nestled, hiding wildflower fields
singing our futures to sun and to wind
guitar notes like bird-songs
on untouched land.

our weariness found us, found us aching for rest-
until we saw, upon a hill, a house left behind same as us.

ignored and neglected, it had grown very ill
hungry and bitter and doors locked up tight
acne over drywall, swollen flesh under drains,
lesions in the baseboards and feverish strain.
yet each flip of a light switch left the darkness uneasy
each step on the floor left the boards craving memory

and when we brought our smiles, our care and our joy
nothing seemed quite the same as before.
the walls grew their flowers, lemonade in the fridge
and we partied all night
as the house settled in.

What can I do to make it go away?

Please, please

It hurts so badly. It aches.

Who do I ask to

make it go away

What can I do to make it go away?

Here are instructions for burying a loved one.

1. Load the body into your car. If you need help (as sometimes bodies are heavy) ask a friend.

2. Drive to a cemetery. You will need a shovel, but if you prefer to use your hands, be my guest. Hands are our God-given tools, after all.

3. Dig.

4. Dig more. That's not deep enough.

5. There you go. It's cold out here, isn't it? Did you bring a jacket? Your cheeks look flushed, and your nose is running. You're just going to wipe it on your sleeve? You don't have tissues or anything?

6. Fine. Drag the body over and dump it in. Start covering it with dirt. If it moves, pretend you didn't see anything. You didn't see that. It's not moving.

7. Go home.

This has been; grief.

fester and rot, skin and bone
my bed is a grave
and I have buried myself in blankets of dirt
I have found a meadow in a field far away
and I have found a tree
who sings me songs in milky sunlight
my shovel has been bound to my hand, so I dig
rot and fester, bone and skin
my bed is a grave and I want to sleep
let me sleep.

Ticket

4

SKELETONIZATION

Hey, it's here! You've made it!
You are finally
becoming your bones.
Doesn't it feel great?
You finally got rid of all that useless, gunky flesh. It was pretty gross when that blood-foam started leaking from your various holes and your body swelled up and liquefied. It was… certainly something. Happens to everyone, though. No need to be embarrassed. But you don't have to worry about that anymore. In fact, you don't have to worry about anything anymore. Isn't that great?
Say it. Say that it's great.
Okay. Good.

Let's get started.

He is mad for her
He wants to take her apart piece by piece and lick the blood from her knuckles, bandage her wounds, worship the dirt her feet have had the grace of touching. Grow crops from it and consume her that way, turning the potatoes and corn into stew and even feeding it to her. Is she not delicious?
What he wouldn't do for her,
It's unimaginable.

static

REPORTER: Good morning, [YOUR MIND]! Welcome to your local news station. I hope you're holding up alright. It seems like your decomposition is coming along nicely- make sure to leave a five-star review for your grave digger. It's probably a depressing job, and they might need cheering up.

There's a new building in town. No one knows what's it's for, exactly, since there aren't any signs, or people, inside. The construction crew hasn't finished with it, but I don't think they ever will, because it's been almost a month and no one has seen any construction workers anywhere. There are pipes, oddly shaped, sticking out of an incomplete brick wall. I have to look at them every time I take my walk in the morning. What an eyesore!

You know, one person, they could look at those pipes and think, hey, pipes! Which is what I normally do. They could also look at them and think, hey, these metal veins pump water through the building and when I drink from water fountains, I taste blood, and get the vague sense that the walls are breathing. They could think something like that- but I'd be careful.

We should all be careful about what we think.

Even My Bones

I want to be a daughter to my mother
Laughing over things we both understand
The things
women
understand

I wish I could talk to her like those girls in the movies
Curling their fingers around telephone cords
Talking and talking.
I wish we could relate but I am separate, untied,
untethered
Floating among space-rock and stars in a daze
Hesitant to carry out the duties a woman must carry out
Nothing like she was, at my age.

I want to be a daughter to my mother
Laughing over things we both understand
the things women understand
I just
don't know
if I can.

Even My Bones

To be understood
It is meaningfully, beautifully pleasurable.

Red red red red red red
Don't look at me, don't look, don't make promises,
promise me, promise me, promise me-

Our codes seem to align.
Our breathing seems to match, our habits known, our
mannerisms reflective. I have been skinned before you.

I hate this. I hate this. I hate this.
I am a doe sighted by a scope, in the line of fire, but can
you draw me a line for affection?

I am more lacking
than you think
and the absence hurts
more than you know.

Alone?

Really? I don't think so. You should check again.

…

You're sure? Positive?

Mmmm… that's not right. Get up. Look under that greasy pizza box, inside the pillows, behind the curtain. Keep the curtain open and scan the empty street outside, biting your lower lip in increasing anxiety, eyes darting back and forth between the orderly streetlamps and trimmed bushes.

Alone? Want to be?

No. No, we never want to be.

I took comfort in them. In memories, too.
I didn't realize I took it for granted until I left
I didn't realize how much I wanted to hear the snores of
my brother in the bedroom adjacent, or the creak of the
stairs late at night, the wear of a house we lived in.
Perhaps I did feel trapped
I was trying
To force myself back in the door
I didn't fit anymore.
I am too big, I cry. I am too big,
I am too big for this place.
I didn't fit on my dad's shoulders, or in my mom's arms
And even worse, I didn't *want* to.
My baby blanket was rags.
To think I once was wrapped in it like
A universe had swallowed me whole.

Even My Bones

I feel the itch of something beneath my senses,
the itch of my bones, bones, bones
and I know it's not evil,
this itch of my bones.

He tastes- *ethereal*- you cannot get enough.
You bite his tongue and he has the audacity to laugh,
a deep rumble that fills your head with lofty implications, with desire.
You ask why he is laughing, fondly.
The lights are low but you strain your eyes to keep looking at the stubble on his jaw, the wine-stain of his lips, the tousled locks of his hair. You are lucky.
"When you bite," he says, grinning, "Bite to bleed."

Even My Bones

Captain, tell me tales of old
wild adventures, brave and bold
melt beneath a space-sun
how to keep your feet, when all you do is run?
a million jade blossoms on a fleet of bouquets
space-cowboy, space smiles, space gun ray
fly me away (fly me to the moon)
time is gone all too soon.
I've got an eye on you, Captain, so don't you forget
kiss me with a lip that's split
let's take a ride and see what's here
hold your hat when the wind gusts rear
like ships on the wind
ships on the wind
hold your hat, we're gonna be
ships on the wind.

Even my bones ache
I laugh. I am too young for that.
The old man laughs.
He says,
I am too young for that.
Yes, I think.

static

REPORTER: Good morning, [YOUR MIND]! Welcome to your local news station on this strange, and confusing, start to the day.

Today, a visiting stranger is bothering customers at Ribcage Coffee Shop. She allegedly jumped up from her computer, spilled her caramel latte all over the floor, and started rambling. "My bones!" she cried, pulling her hair. "My bones are upset with me! They're upset that I'm fighting, and there's nothing I can do!"
This commotion was upsetting to the customers and the stranger was asked to leave. She did, if reluctantly, though she was still screaming about her bones as they led her outside.

On this case, one of our sources headed out to consult the expertise of a resident doctor on the matter, Doctor Almond.
"Bones?" he said, confused. "Why are you asking about bones? They're perfectly normal to have."
"Can you tell me more?" Our source asked.
"Our bones are fine," he warned. "Stop talking about them! I don't know anything weird about them and if I did I wouldn't be allowed to talk about it anyway!"

The other doctors we asked responded similarly, shooting us wary glances and mumbling about the press.

You're sixty-six years old.
Orange juice tastes fuzzy and upsets your stomach. Everything upsets your stomach. You take your other half to the park and you feed the ducks together. Your brother is moving to the city and you'll be able to see him more. This makes you happy. Ever since the baby grew up and left for school, you felt lonely, and empty, staring at the bed where you used to kiss them goodnight.
Rip, rip, goes the bread.
The ducks quack.
Quack, quack, go the ducks.
Your skin is wrinkly, and you don't remember things as well as you used to, but today it is nice, and there are flowers growing along the sidewalk. Maybe you'll go out for dinner together. Have a glass of wine.
Quack, quack.

I wonder if I will have cancer like my mother

…

I think this would be inconvenient.

I think that the world is very big and space is very vast and the stars have better things to do than watch me rot away in a hospital bed with IV strings in my veins. The stars are probably far more preoccupied with other things, like the football game. Or tectonic plates.

I want to float up there. As far from anything as anything else, and have an epiphany like philosophers who sat wine-drunk in white temples in robes.

I think an epiphany would also be inconvenient.

If the stars have to watch me suffer cancer

I will make sure

They hear my non-existent revelations every night.

newsboys scream that green hair is the rage
because it makes us look like moss,
there's an onion-mushroom burger on sale
at the restaurant down the street
and the cheese-moon melts
when we point our cameras at it.

[PATRICK] Everything in me is collapsing. Everything in me is so breakable that I question if it's even there at all. Is there anything in there? Oh God, I want to shake myself and ask, is anything in there?

[GOD] Organs. I hear they're in demand, right now.

[PATRICK] That doesn't matter! Are you even listening?

[GOD] Of course. But it is more complicated than that, isn't it? I don't have ears. I don't have eyes. I don't have anything. I am you, and the flowers you're standing on, and the deer you killed and ate. All the time. Everywhere. How am I supposed to know if you are empty? How am I supposed to know if that the emptiness belongs to you?

[PATRICK] So when I die, what then? Will I know if I'm more than my body? Am I more than this?

[GOD] You misunderstand me. I do not know, Patrick. I do not know if you are empty or not. But I think I know what you are really asking. And I think my answer is yes.

he is sailing somewhere
on a boat made of wooden planks and nails
the salty ocean takes him somewhere. An island, maybe.
maybe there are golden-haired princes with swords, or
animals who can make wishes, or grass that sings.
even my bones think
that this sounds nice.

Even My Bones

This poetry sounds young
I can hear it in my words, because I know I am young.
The world has many more dishes for me to sample.
Fancy, raw, digging my fork into sauce and steaming
meat. Draining soup from the bowl. Sucking sugared
candy and ice cream until the only remnants are the
stickiness of my fingers.
There's no rush, though. I myself am a dish
eaten slowly, eventually,
licked off the fingers of the universe.

I don't think I've ever felt so unbearably alone. I wonder how the people in my life, past tense, are doing. If they miss my company, and jokes. Did I make jokes? Someone knocks on the door and I ignore it, because I'm picturing a bear in a suit pinning up an eviction notice.

My bed is warm, the sheets are not clean, and the fan above my head is constantly running. Whir, whir. It sounds like the droning I'd sometimes hear from the dishwasher late at night, though not nearly as loud. It bothers me.

I play cards with myself. So far, I've only won a few matches. The daylight burns scars into headaches. I'm young. I'm twenty- I'm twenty- eight? Nine. My name.

My name is...

She's standing on the side of the road, there is blood
caked on her palms that mixes with the dust of dunes
It's alright, she thinks
Wind reminds her that cloth is not skin
The car is unmoving (cars usually move- but not today)
There is no past, here, no future
The strum of an electric guitar echoes across canyons
and western wilds, red and chilling, to catch in the gap
between her lips like a kiss.

The hood of the truck is blanket-covered and sunken, slightly, beneath the weight of our bodies. I don't know how many bodies- the truck was only so big, mind you, but we all tried to fit. Didn't want to leave anyone out. Some of them sat on the roof, sneakers dangling over the windshield above my head. One of them nudged my face with their shoe, and I laughed, giggled, these sounds emerging from my mouth as birdlings emerge from cracking shells. Stargazing, watching those specks of light so intently as if they were going to disappear, as if they were going to twinkle out of existence. Someone has a book on their lap and is pointing out the constellations. Cepheus, Ursa Minor, Auriga. Pegasus, Andromeda, Lyra. I would have heard more but my vision was darkening, my cheek pressed into a shoulder and my arm around a waist, and soon the only stars I was seeing were behind my eyelids.

Even my bones are cooked
I'm laid out on plates, quartered and sectioned, eye
rolling in a glass of chestnut-and-cranberry scented red
wine. They mean to eat me, I think lazy, still rolling.
They mean to devour.
My hand is curled and buttered like crab, leg in a
barbeque roast, blood-marinade and organ delicacies.
Someone idly grabs a fork, and like the time I screamed
my way out of a dark womb,
It begins.

WHY

DON'T

YOU

CARE?

WHY

DON'T

YOU

SEE?

The TV flickers awake, awash in static and glitching patterns. You sit on the carpet patiently, wooden blocks scattered in front of you- but your attention is quite obviously fixed on the screen.

"Hello, friends!"

The cartoon doctor looks at you. She has large ears, and big, wide eyes. She's in a hospital, wearing a white surgical coat and a stethoscope around her neck.

"Today we're going to be doctors!"

She gestures to the patient, dressed in a hospital gown and half-awake. They blink, confused, from their spot on the operating table.

"Oh no, look! Our friend has covered up all their bones!" The doctor shakes her head and puts her hands on her hips. "We have a scalpel, a saw, or scissors! Which one do *you* think we should we use?"

She looks into your eyes as she waits for you to answer. It's a drawn-out pause. It grows longer than it should, and you understand you need to do something.

You point to the one in the middle, the scalpel.

"Good choice! I *love* it!" She squeals, grinning. So wide. So terribly, terribly wide. Her eyes. Her smile.

You nod, agreeing.

She winks. "The bones will love it, too."

There's a fire-watch tower in the woods. Far away from wherever you live. Unless *you* live in the woods. Then, maybe, not so far.

He leans on the railing, watching endless hills of dark pines mingle in loss and deceit, whisper of flames to the west. The man can smell it- the smoke, in the air. He inhales in like he inhales the scent of his quilted bedsheets, his grandpa's old shirt, an empty perfume bottle. There is something down there, at the base of his tower. The man looks at it.

Red eyes.

Evil in the woods.

There is an understanding between them. Pine needles crunch and wind creaks the tower, the burn of hot coffee still on his tongue, still crusting the bottom of the pot, still dried on the edge of a ceramic mug inside. He sees the red reflect in his own gaze and he smiles, waving.

The mysterious evil waves back.

And the trees,

they whisper.

Hold me with bloodied hands.

[GOD] Why is it so important for you to plead forgiveness? Why? You are one lifeform out of billions, trillions. Uncountable. What is guilt to the universe? What is guilt to God?

PATRICK stares blankly at the milk as it swirls in his coffee, a splendid mix of cream white and mud brown, soil and clouds kissing in his mug.

[PATRICK] You don't get it. You just… don't get it.

His voice was a whisper.

PATRICK looks up at GOD, something like hatred hiding behind his watery eyes.

The seeds are melting, she says, hand on her straw hat because it was going to fly away. Blue freckles form on her cheeks like whiskey raindrops. I look at the garden.
The seeds are melting.
What do we do? I ask, panic on the edge of my wild throat, canopied by willow leaves that stretch into my guts.
You stole their water, she says. Did they see you?
I don't know. They don't have eyes, but they look at me, and I feel like they've already slammed the judge's hammer- reverberating guilty, guilty, guilty.
I was just so thirsty.

don't pity me

pity is for the weak

and even if I am

don't remind me of it.

Do you know love?
The sun is rising, and the dawn is ahead- I feel simultaneously like a carcass and a newborn, like I'm rotting and like I've just come screaming into the world with rosy cheeks still tethered to my mother.

Do you know love?
I feel it in the riptide of gem-washed wind, glittering light through glass- I feel the bark of the tree wrap her arms around the skin of my youth, I feel my eyes burn of a life I have not yet had the privilege of living and have lived for a hundred years.

Do you know love?
I feel crisped like I've been stuck in a pot of oil, turned about until I am edible, until I crack and crinkle and crumb. I feel withered as the tulips come to be in autumn but will I not be there when spring comes again? When my lips are watered and my parched throat clenches around the cold, quenching life I am fed?

Do you know love?

RAT lays down in his cot. "We have a big show tomorrow," he says, itching his whiskers. "Big show."
I pull up my quilt to my nose- it is musty and old and the colors have lived in it for quite a while. I breathe in the dust mites and think of a response.
"I don't dream," I mumble. "I don't dream all the time and I wonder if I'm real."
"*Mmmmm*," RAT says. "The show is real."
"I don't care about the show."
RAT huffs. "We all care about the show."
Here, the boxcar is filled with hay, and the morning sun is already rising. It's warm and bright over the hills.
"Rise and Shine!" the sun shouts,
in a language that we all understand.
"But we haven't even slept yet!" I argue, distraught.
Still, RAT leaps to his paws, and starts getting ready.

There is tension here. Tension, tied in sideways glances and muttered insults. Not easily as cut as butter. The butter would have to be frozen, that's how heavy it was. The tension.
This is a funny comparison, I think.
The butter thinks it is funny, too.
The butter knife slumps.
It has its work
cut out for it.

Growing boy, they whisper hungrily.

Growing, growing boy.

I turn my head. No one is there. Only the sidewalk, and the streetlights, and my hands tucked into the pockets of my hoodie. No one.

Growing boyyyyyyyyyy

I turn around in time to see a group of kids sneak up behind me and dump a bucket on my head- I had thought it to be water, but I did not feel the icy prank I was expecting. Instead, it was warm, and thicker, and white, and smelled very strong. Milk. It was milk.

The kids laughed and bolted into the night. The streetlamp flickered. I stood there, dripping wet and indescribably warm.

Growing boy, they whispered. *Growing, growing boy.*

Perhaps I am guilty.

211

Even My Bones

Here are instructions for going swimming.

1. Buy a bathing suit. My, my, there's quite a lot of options, aren't there? That's a horrible shade of green. Get a different one.

2. Put the bathing suit on, but don't look in the mirror. In fact, you really shouldn't have a mirror in your house at all.

3. Find water. Water is in a lot of places, some of them big enough for swimming, so I'll leave that to you. You're not an idiot. Take out your phone and look up your local pool, or rec center.

4. Now you're standing at the water. Your toes are just dipping into the edge, and it feels cold. You can't see the bottom. You blink, thinking it's your eyesight, but nope- there really is no bottom. Are you sure you want to be doing this?

5. The water wraps around you like air does, but this is thicker, and heavier. Your arms splash in panic, your feet kicking desperately. You try to read these instructions but you left them on the bench over there. Isn't that unlucky?

6. Breathe. I don't care that it's water, breathe it in. Something's got a hold on your ankle. Let it drag you. There's only bubbles, left, now.

This has been; swimming.

[PATRICK] You foresaw this. You foresaw me.

[GOD] I foresee everything.

[PATRICK] And everyone.

[GOD] Yes.

… there is a pause. A lengthy pause, a pause no one can tell the length of because it could have been years, or minutes, or seconds, and it was the world and it was not, and it was real and it was not, and it was love, and it was not.

[PATRICK] Are you here? Am I dreaming?

GOD does not respond.

She lays tangled in bedsheets. Blankets, and quilts. Warmth drapes through the window and she rolls over, settling, blinking blearily at the sunlit leaves that move in waves together- summer green right outside.
An alarm clock is at her bedside.
She doesn't have to listen to it, today. Or tomorrow, even- even though she has grown up. She is a grown-up.
She doesn't think about what she *has* to do today but what she *will* do today, because ahead there is a vast bright vision of nothing, and she figures she will probably fill it with something.
There are clothes on the floor, and action figures on the desk. Posters, and headphones, and beautiful teenage wreckage returning to a childhood bedroom.
Perhaps there is an end
There is an end to all things
But it feels far, and insignificant, like the stripe of cloud an airplane leaves behind in the sky.

am I delusional for thinking
there is a monster in me
there is blood in the morsels
blood in the tea
blood in the man with the beard by the sea.
blood between nails
blood on my knees
am I delusional for thinking
there's a monster in me?

My head is clearer.

Another blood moon came, though when I went to the white tree, still standing wretched and warped, the bear was gone. It woke up from its slumber. The mushroom I'd managed to preserve became like golden dust in its glass jar. I'm not sure what it means, but I am happy. I think it's good. I think I wasn't meant to be messing around with things like that, anyway. The bear, it must be tired of me bothering him all the time. Maybe it's tired of bothering me. I'll leave the woods alone for a while.

Spring is here. Everything is blooming. I think the bear moved on. Maybe to a different town, a different woods, a different person. But I think it's going to be okay, now.

I think it's going to be okay.

You are eighty-nine years old.
You've discovered the wonders of mindless, motionless
television- painted yellows, and greens, and blues.
Even red.
There's an itch on your leg, but you can't reach it. Your
baby is in the other room on the phone, and the sun is
large, and you can't understand her voice because you're
so tired. If you could, you would know that she's saying,
*"I just don't know what to do. I don't know. What do I
do, start planning funeral arrangements? It's so hard to
deal with I can't even think about it. It's so hard."*
But you don't know that, you silly goose.
You don't know anything. You're eighty-nine.
And the sun is very large.

Even My Bones

perched on a bridge

two birds, otherwise empty

one white, one black

one on each side like idle gate guards standing at their

posts, beady eyes observing

an arch beyond

surround by sea.

static

REPORTER: Good morning, [YOUR MIND]! Welcome to your local news station. Truthfully, I don't know how much longer I'll be able to be on air. Tough times loom on the striking, moonless horizon. Well, basically moonless. It's only a crescent right now, but we all know that's a bad time of the cycle.

Something is… winning. An enemy. War is hard and war is here. The office-supply employees have vacated their store. A lot of people are scared, but some aren't. And you- you're almost there. It's all coming down in a great, cataclysmic end. Is it the right thing, to be scared right now? To be boarding up your windows and stocking up on apocalypse supplies? I don't know. No one knows anything. Maybe ask the fish.

The winds are high, and the crops are not growing. They decided to go on strike because Farmer Kimmick isn't giving them enough water. They claim that he stole it from them, and that it's all rightfully theirs, but Farmer Kimmick argues that he needs at least a little bit to make his tea in the morning.

The seeds scream their agony.

Even My Bones

Do not dwell on idle things,
the things I was before
My sins and all my sorrows,
they're knocking on my door.
the sun hangs high, in judgement
shaking hands of guilt
my heart is in the doorway,
my mind of wayward tilt.
The eye of God, it watches,
singed in ripened glare
My sins and all my sorrows
are all too much to bear.

Is blood red? Is it blue? Are bones really as breakable as they look? Do they look like toothpicks? Do they look like cotton swabs? Are you bones yet? Are you bones?

"How was your day?" you ask
and I think, you are tired. you are holding your keys at
the door and your shoes are still on and you had to work
and you are tired.
My mouth gapes open and close like a fish out of water.
The fish opens its mouth and gapes, even though it is in
water, in a bowl, on the counter.
"Good," I say, because it was. There is no other answer.
There is no other possible state of day. "Good."

He is dancing a waltz
You have him by the waist, you bloody him
And he is
enthralled

Converge on the shores of beaches that don't exist (it's a sandbox) and bury your hands deep, deep down- to your wrists, elbows, shoulders. You must scream, and scream loudly as sweat runs down your forehead, as your sleep-shirt sticks to your chest in midnight summer heat, as worms crawl from their murky soil only to be snatched away by a very, very, *very* early bird. Scream. Scream raw and uncoiled by the restraints of your routine. Scream like you don't have to wake up at six tomorrow. Scream and pretend that you matter before the clocks unwind like a bouncing yo-yo string and converge on beaches that don't exist.

And eventually we are all there at the station, waving goodbye. Hair in the breeze. The grass is green and the clouds stuff themselves with sunshine. A train whistle blows. We tried to pack them all in our tiny leather briefcase- the ones we loved-
But they couldn't fit. That's alright. It's not the last time you'll ever see each other.
You have another train to catch
And it was nice to have company while you waited.

let's watch the planets crumble together- under a sky like
a ripe, bursting peach, endless violet space above
sit on top of an old diner, we are not
touching
but I know you're there
we are not talking
but I can hear the quiet crimson rhythm of your lungs
we are not looking at one another
but I hope you know I still love you
my sneakers are swinging off the roof
and my bones are tired, lopsided gears
and the wind is tenderly brushing my hair as mothers do
and I am happy.

Blow a kiss to a shooting star, make a wish
So that when you lay your head on a fluffy pillow
You will be safe (protected); loved.

I am on a plane. It is nighttime.
I place my hands to the small, cold window and press my face to the double-paned glass. It is wonderful.
And the lights, bright and glittering like fairy dust in the dark, twinkling from so far below.
I can almost hear the music.
There is music, I am sure of it.
The airplane whirrs its great static in the sky and I blink- here it comes- the cliff. Of course, I know that under me is only the ocean, and the lights on the coast,
but this evades me spectacularly.
The lights stop so finally, right upon the cliff's edge, and give way to void. A void containing everything and nothing, consuming in its entirety. I cannot see the lapping waves nor below… it is black. It is void.
Void, void.
For a moment I picture outer space, that this is what it would be like to float among stars like astronauts on the yellowed covers of comics, and elegant piano playing the symphony of my departure.
That this is what death would feel like.
Void.

It has consumed me, I am constricted torturously by the
hand of bitter ills. Blood spills like sweet grape juice and
I raise my head to see death on the horizon.
Spare me, I beg
A whisper only for the weeping clouds, the dirt, the rust
covering my metal shell
I am not spared.
It's not like that, the roots think, and I
awaken in a wasteland
as robots paint my fingernails.

Even My Bones

Are you aware
that the rise and fall of your chest
under my head
is the ebb and tide of blood, and flesh
I can hear your heart and it is singing to me like an old
record player sings- you have never been more alive than
when I can hear the proof of it
thump, thump, thump
like little rabbit feet
run run little rabbit, run faster and faster, beat so heavily
that my eardrum begins to sting and bleed out onto your
shirt, until it's all I can hear and there's nothing else in
the entire world that could deafen me so-

I made pie today. The cherry one you always liked when you came over, and my Mom would pull it right out of the oven. Red syrup, sweet tang- our tongues were so happy. We were so easy to please. I wonder if you remember.

The day is bright. I walked out of the house, into the street, and I had to shield my eyes. The wind is chipper, and fresh. The sky is blue. A few feet away, a boy falls on his bicycle. He curses- he's skinned his knee. And I think, this is a new start. Summer, you know?

I ran over to help.

The fish is rotting but I cut into it anyway. I caught it, I say angrily, ripping apart the scales so they stick to my hands, slimy and wet. I caught it, didn't I? I rip and rip and rip until there is nothing left but scraps, and I realize that my mother is inside cooking potatoes with red-pepper-flakes and butter in a pot and my father is setting the table, and I am here, beyond them, beyond their warm window, standing in my muddy fishing boots with nothing to put on their plates.

I only watch as a hawk swoops down from above. We look at one another, beak to nose, bristling feathers to sweaty skin. When I don't shoo it away, it pecks at the bits and pieces I'd thrown about, and I feel my boots sink a little further down into the mud.

Here are instructions for taking care of flowers.

1. Plant the seeds in fertile soil. Give them plenty of water, so they are never thirsty.

2. Sunlight is important for healthy growth. Tell the sun to shine on them. Louder! The sun can't hear you if you don't yell.

3. Wait. Wait years. Years and years. Foster them and love them with everything you have. Their petals have never been so colorful.

4. You are old. You are so, so old. Your hair is grey- maybe it's already gone. The flowers are wilting. Well, what are you waiting for? Do something! They're leaving you! Oh, Emily, what did I do? I love you! Don't go!

5. Sit. Cry.

6. Cry for a long, *long* time.

This has been; children.

Life is hard, you say, between sips of cola.
The straw is striped white and red. It turns darker, when
you drink. *Life is so, so hard.*
And it is, I'm sure.
I live second-hand through your life all the time.
You just never seem to ask
about mine.

He takes a long, long look. I think perhaps he is praying but there is blood between his clasped hands and blood on his collar and blood, wrapped ever so tightly, around his bones. I watch. I will be late, but I watch. He's praying over a cereal box under a cerulean sky on an evening that is pleasant because it is not raining- but I can smell the rain coming and there is a satisfaction in the knowing, a satisfaction in the rain, in the cerulean of the sky. He stops mumbling and smashes the box. *Crunch. Crunch.* His ragged untied sneakers are the lords of destruction. When it is finished, and cereal is spread all over the sidewalk, he stands up calmly and walks away. Blood on his hands. Blood on his collar. Blood, wrapped ever so tightly, around his bones.

[PATRICK] My boss fired me today. Said I was too distracted to be doing what park rangers do. Too distracted to range in the parks, and all.

[GOD] …

[PATRICK] They're worried about me. The town is worried, the crops are worried, even the radio is worried. But I'm not. I'm not. I feel better than I have in a long time.

PATRICK takes a seat on his porch. A sparrow flutters nearby, and perches on a wire, observing. Nothing is everything and everything is nothing and the teapot inside finishes boiling, the bubbles grow shallower, until there aren't any more bubbles at all.

[PATRICK] I am so happy it's over.

The crops are red, the crops are blue, the spaceship hovers over him in a way that blocks out the stars, and the cornfield is in the spotlight.

Red, blue, waves like the northern lights and his hair is astray and his jacket is blown open to the universe. Red, blue. Think of arcade games and 80's sci-fi magazines that claim that lizards live under our cities. Red, blue. Think of the farmer down the street, his curtains illuminated, his mouth open in a half-snore while his wife wakes up and stares, stares at the light, and in her hazy state thinks she is dreaming. Red, blue. Think of what hides in the corn and behind gas stations at night and in the backseat of your car.

Think, always, all of the time.

Red, blue.

I have felt love- it resides in the laughter I hear- sounds uncontrolled and unrestrained. Midnight suns spiral, purple comets and UFO glimpses. Gimmick lights. Flushed cheeks, show your teeth, spill your drink. Touch my shoulder to remind me I'm real, and point- look-
oh, look at that.
Look at the stars, you say.
Look at what they're telling us.
You smile.
We must be connected,
because I can't control my own.

The bear looks down at you with a tilt of its head. You've sunken down so that the soil hugs your sides. You turn your head and see a ladybug climb over a stem of grass. It is the most beautiful thing you've ever seen.

The bear curls up beside you, and you close your eyes.

Do you believe in destiny? I ask,
And our conversation is as it always is, our words flow,
gentle touches, friendship. Sunlight is so warm on our
hands. Destiny gives me some kind of hope.

These silver ships will carry us home.
Are you happy? Are you happy where we are? Oh, look
at all the flowers these valleys have nurtured. Look at the
rust-tinged soil beneath our feet that gives way to the
horizon ahead of us. Dance with me, even if you're tired.
Even if your bones want to rest- resist! Resist and stand!
Dance with me! Dance! The answers reveal only more
questions and honestly, that's okay. It's more okay than
anything will ever be.

Do you believe in destiny? I ask, and stretch out my
hand. Please. My bones want to dance.

My bones want to dance.

Let go.

I don't want to. I don't want to let go.

It's time.

It's not.

It is, and the words are kind.
The words are gentle.
Death is gentle.
It is.

static

REPORTER: Good night, [YOUR MIND]. Thank you so much for listening to the local news station. Thank you so much for dying.

I leave you with a message, from the cult of *The Sacred Iris*. They say that the enemy is appeased, for now, but will be requesting more ring pops in the future. Thankfully, the future can never come because it's always ahead of us, and that's a long time from now.

Resident Doctor Almond has assured us that the problem with the bones has been resolved. We told him that we weren't even aware of a problem, and he shook his head, waving us away. Doctors are strange, sometimes.

The weather is going to be clear, and sunny tomorrow. The trees are going to sing one of the new songs from *The Peeled-Grape Cowboy's* new album, and the crops have agreed to leave some of the water for us.

And hey, ask your Pops if he can take the day off work-it'll be a nice day to go fishing.

Even My Bones

Before I went to college
My mother took me to the top of a mountain
Where flowers kissed above the world, and the water
was so far from the heart of the earth
that it froze my fingertips.
She rested next to me, and we made a story together.

I remembered when I would sleep beside her, younger
When I was sick and aching
and she rubbed my back in circles,
slipped medicine past my dry lips that called out to her in
in the turmoil of night when she didn't want to be awake
And even younger
When I was small enough to fit in her lap
And I wasn't old enough to make stories yet
But she could read them to me.

I wish I could lay there beside her, again
for a while.

my brain is pink and spoiled
a pig roast off the spit
it all feels weak and boiled
can't conjure any wit.
perhaps the sun is lucky
it's married to the moon
I lay my brain with reverence
and scoop it with a spoon.

You stand victorious.

Sweat plasters your forehead, soaks your shirt. Air, mist, clarity. Honey drips from your limbs, sliding off as if only a memory, a dream. You stand over the corpse of the tree. It is nothing but ash, now, flowing in the breeze over a grey withered stump. The organs are gone.

They're *gone*.

The axe falls from your hands, clumps onto the grass and sinks slowly beneath the dirt. The glaring red above you fades. It fades, everything seems to change- the sun against a crisp blue sky and green, lovely grass. A cool breeze. Someone's calling your name, in the woods. It's distant, but it's there. You turn to the forest.

You turn to the forest, and you don't look back.

Did you have a good time?
I sure hope you did. It took a while, but we're here.
It's done.
The angels are singing (with a particularly good guitarist), a tree writhing with mysterious organs has been slain, and most importantly, someone, maybe you, drank the milk.
The bones nod.
The bones are all you have left.
The bones are satisfied,
and they let go.

[GOD] You look sick.

[PATRICK] I am always sick, now, God.

The monitor BEEPS loudly. BEEP. BEEP.

[GOD] I made you like this. I made you, so it's going to be okay. I am the Almighty, and I know these things.

[PATRICK] You made me? All of me? My dry eyes, my tender muscles, my aching stomach? Even my illness?

GOD smiles.

[GOD] Even your bones.

[END]

AUTHOR's NOTE

Wow! You made it!

I hope you thought it was wonderful.

This was one of my favorite collections to write. It was bloody, and terrible, and emotional. It was confusing, and weird. It was human. I dug deep into the spot under my ribs, right beneath my heart, where I feel like my soul is. One of my friends asked me that- where I thought my soul was. I had never thought about it before. Is it in the back of your mouth, where your words flow? The spot where your headaches persist? Maybe it's the sole of your foot.

Anyway, I was thinking about that a lot.

I like to think I've matured over the past few years, as I've grown, entering my early twenties. Some might say that's not very old. Some, like the kids I tend to babysit, would say that I'm practically a dinosaur.

I try not to think about how old I am too much, because it scares me. When I think about these things for too long, they always scare me. I try not to be scared because I need to take the time I've been given as a gift. Recently I've been overwhelmed with gratitude for it. I really don't want to waste it. It's going to be scary, to take risks, but I have to. It's my way of saying thank you.

I wrote this because, like most people, I've got emotions and I need a way to focus them. Hone them in. Understand them. Mostly, though, I just think it's fun to put my effort into something I love. To make something sickening, and beautiful, and strange. Something lasting. I wonder if God felt the same way making us.

Such is the joy of creation.

www.ingramcontent.com/pod-product-compliance
Lightning Source LLC
Chambersburg PA
CBHW020754310726
48969CB00002B/536